PENGUIN CLASSICS

Maigret and the Tramp

'Extraordinary masterpieces of the twentieth century'
– John Banville

'A brilliant writer' – India Knight

'Intense atmosphere and resonant detail . . . make Simenon's fiction remarkably like life' – Julian Barnes

'A truly wonderful writer . . . marvellously readable – lucid, simple, absolutely in tune with the world he creates'
– Muriel Spark

'Few writers have ever conveyed with such a sure touch, the bleakness of human life' – A. N. Wilson

'Compelling, remorseless, brilliant' – John Gray

'A writer of genius, one whose simplicity of language creates indelible images that the florid stylists of our own day can only dream of' – *Daily Mail*

'The mysteries of the human personality are revealed in all their disconcerting complexity' – Anita Brookner

'One of the greatest writers of our time' – *The Sunday Times*

'I love reading Simenon. He makes me think of Chekhov'
– William Faulkner

'One of the great psychological novelists of this century'
– *Independent*

'The greatest of all, the most genuine novelist we have had in literature' – André Gide

'Simenon ought to be spoken of in the same breath as Camus, Beckett and Kafka' – *Independent on Sunday*

ABOUT THE AUTHOR

Georges Simenon was born on 12 February 1903 in Liège, Belgium, and died in 1989 in Lausanne, Switzerland, where he had lived for the latter part of his life. Between 1931 and 1972 he published seventy-five novels and twenty-eight short stories featuring Inspector Maigret.

Simenon always resisted identifying himself with his famous literary character, but acknowledged that they shared an important characteristic:

> My motto, to the extent that I have one, has been noted often enough, and I've always conformed to it. It's the one I've given to old Maigret, who resembles me in certain points . . . 'Understand and judge not'.

Penguin is publishing the entire series of Maigret novels.

GEORGES SIMENON

Maigret and the Tramp

Translated by HOWARD CURTIS

PENGUIN BOOKS

PENGUIN CLASSICS

UK | USA | Canada | Ireland | Australia
India | New Zealand | South Africa

Penguin Books is part of the Penguin Random House group of companies
whose addresses can be found at global.penguinrandomhouse.com.

First published in French as *Maigret et le Clochard* by Presses de la Cité, 1963
This translation first published 2018
002

Copyright © Georges Simenon Limited, 1963
Translation copyright © Howard Curtis, 2018
GEORGES SIMENON ® Simenon.tm
MAIGRET ® Georges Simenon Limited
All rights reserved

The moral rights of the author and translator have been asserted

Set in 12.5/15 pt Dante MT Std
Typeset by Jouve (UK), Milton Keynes
Printed and bound in Great Britain by Clays Ltd, Elcograf S.p.A.

ISBN: 978–0–241–30399–3

www.greenpenguin.co.uk

Penguin Random House is committed to a
sustainable future for our business, our readers
and our planet. This book is made from Forest
Stewardship Council® certified paper.

Maigret and the Tramp

1.

There was a moment, between Quai des Orfèvres and Pont Marie, when Maigret paused, so briefly that Lapointe, who was walking beside him, paid no attention. And yet, for a few seconds, perhaps only a split second, Maigret had been taken back to when he was his companion's age.

It was doubtless something to do with the quality of the air, its luminosity, its smell, its taste. There had been a morning just like this, mornings just like this, in the days when, as a young inspector newly appointed to the Police Judiciaire, which Parisians still called the Sûreté, Maigret worked the beat, tramping the streets of Paris from morning to night.

Although it was already 25 March, this was the first real day of spring, all the more limpid for the fact that there had been a last shower during the night, accompanied by distant rolls of thunder. It was also the first time in the year that Maigret had left his overcoat in his office cupboard, and from time to time the breeze caused his unbuttoned jacket to billow.

Because of this whiff of the past, he had, without realizing it, adopted his old pace, neither slow nor fast, not quite the pace of someone out for a stroll and stopping to look at the minor sights of the street, nor quite that of someone with a particular purpose in mind.

His hands together behind his back, he looked around him, right, left, up in the air, registering images to which he had not paid any attention for a long time.

For such a short journey, there had been no question of taking one of the black cars lined up in the courtyard of the Police Judiciaire, and the two men were walking by the river. Pigeons flew off as they crossed the square in front of Notre-Dame, where there was already a tourist coach, a big yellow coach from Cologne.

Crossing the iron footbridge, they reached Ile Saint-Louis. In a window, Maigret noticed a young chambermaid in a uniform and a white lace cap, like something from a boulevard comedy. A little further on, a butcher's boy, also in uniform, was delivering meat; a postman was just coming out of an apartment building.

The buds had opened that very morning, dappling the trees with soft green flecks.

'The Seine's still high,' Lapointe remarked. It was the first thing he had said.

It was true. For a month now, it had barely stopped raining, and then only for a few hours. Almost every evening, the television showed swollen rivers and towns and villages with flooded streets. The water of the Seine was yellowish, and carried all kinds of litter, old crates, tree branches along with it.

The two men followed Quai de Bourbon as far as Pont Marie, which they crossed at the same calm pace. Downstream, they could see a greyish barge with the white and red triangle of the Compagnie Générale on its bow. Its name was the *Poitou*, and a crane was unloading sand from its hold, with a wheezing and creaking that mingled with the indistinct noises of the city.

Another barge was moored upstream of the bridge, some fifty metres from the first. It looked cleaner, as if it had been polished that very morning. A Belgian flag fluttered lazily in the stern. Near the white cabin, a baby lay asleep in a hammock-shaped canvas cradle. A very tall man with light-blond hair was looking in the direction of the riverbank, as if waiting for something.

The name of the boat, in gold letters, was *De Zwarte Zwaan*, a Flemish name, which neither Maigret nor Lapointe understood.

It was two or three minutes to ten. The two police officers reached Quai des Célestins. As they descended the ramp to the quayside, a car drew up, and three men got out, slamming the door.

'Ah, we've arrived at the same time!'

They, too, had come from the Palais de Justice, but from the more imposing part reserved for magistrates. There was Deputy Prosecutor Parrain, Examining Magistrate Dantziger and an old clerk of the court whose name Maigret could never remember, even though he had met him hundreds of times.

It wouldn't have occurred to the passers-by on their way to work or the children playing on the pavement opposite that this was an official visit by the prosecutor's office. In the bright morning, there was nothing at all solemn about it. The deputy prosecutor took a gold cigarette case from his pocket and mechanically held it out to Maigret, even though he had his pipe in his mouth.

'Oh, of course, I forgot . . .'

He was a tall, thin, fair-haired man, quite distinguished-looking; it struck Maigret once again that this was characteristic of the prosecutor's office. As for Dantziger, who was short and round, he was plainly dressed. Examining magistrates came in all shapes and sizes. So why did those from the prosecutor's office all look more or less like senior civil servants, with manners, elegance and often arrogance to match?

'Shall we go, gentlemen?'

They walked down the ramp with its uneven cobbles, and came to the quayside, not far from the barge.

'Is this the one?'

Maigret knew no more than they did. He had read in the daily reports a brief account of what had happened during the night and had received a telephone call half an hour earlier, asking him to be present when the prosecutor's men arrived.

He didn't mind. He was back in a world, an atmosphere he had experienced on several occasions. All five men advanced towards the motor barge, which was linked to the quayside by a gangplank, and the tall fair-haired bargee took a few steps towards them.

'Give me your hand,' he said to the deputy prosecutor, who was the first in line. 'To be on the safe side, right?'

His Flemish accent was pronounced. His clear-cut features, his pale eyes, his big arms, his way of moving recalled his country's cyclists being interviewed after a race.

The noise of the crane unloading the sand was louder here.

'Is your name Joseph Van Houtte?' Maigret asked, after glancing at a piece of paper.

'Jef Van Houtte, yes, monsieur.'

'Are you the owner of this boat?'

'Of course I'm the owner, monsieur, who else would be?'

A pleasant smell of cooking rose from the cabin, and at the foot of the staircase, which was covered in flower-patterned linoleum, a very young woman could be seen coming and going.

Maigret pointed to the baby in its cradle.

'Is that your son?'

'Not my son, monsieur, my daughter. Yolande, her name is. My sister's name is also Yolande, she's her godmother.'

Signalling to the clerk of the court to take notes, Deputy Prosecutor Parrain now decided to intervene.

'Tell us what happened.'

'Well, I fished him out, and the skipper on the other boat helped me.'

He pointed to the *Poitou*, in whose stern a man stood leaning against the helm, looking in their direction as if awaiting his turn.

A tugboat sounded its siren several times and passed slowly upstream with four barges behind it. Each time one of them came level with the *Zwarte Zwaan*, Jef Van Houtte raised his arm in greeting.

'Did you know the drowning man?'

'I'd never even seen him before.'

'How long have you been moored here?'

'Since last night. I've come from Jeumont, with a cargo

of slates for Rouen. I was planning to go through Paris and stop for the night at the Suresnes lock. I suddenly noticed that something was wrong with the engine . . . We don't especially like spending the night in the middle of Paris, if you know what I mean.'

In the distance, Maigret saw two or three tramps standing under the bridge, among them a very fat woman he had the feeling he had seen before.

'How did it happen? Did the man jump in the water?'

'I don't think so, monsieur. If he'd jumped in the water, what would the other two be doing here?'

'What time was it? Where were you? Tell us precisely what happened during the evening. You moored here just before nightfall?'

'That's right.'

'Did you notice a tramp under the bridge?'

'You don't notice these things. They're almost always there.'

'What did you do then?'

'We all had dinner, Hubert, Anneke and me.'

'Who's Hubert?'

'My brother. He works with me. Anneke's my wife. Her name's Anna, but we call her Anneke.'

'And then?'

'My brother put on his nice suit and went dancing. At his age, why not?'

'How old is he?'

'Twenty-two.'

'Is he here?'

'He went to buy supplies. He'll be back.'

'What did you do after dinner?'

'I went to work on the engine. I saw right away that there was an oil leak, and as I was planning to leave in the morning I did the repairs.'

He kept darting suspicious glances at each of them in turn, like someone who isn't used to having dealings with the law.

'When did you complete the work?'

'I didn't. I only finished it off this morning.'

'Where were you when you heard the shouting?'

He scratched his head, looking straight ahead at the spacious, gleaming deck.

'First, I came up on deck once to smoke a cigarette and see if Anneke was asleep.'

'What time was that?'

'About ten. I'm not entirely sure.'

'Was she asleep?'

'Yes, monsieur. And the baby was asleep, too. There are nights when she cries, because she's teething.'

'Did you go back to your engine?'

'Of course.'

'Was the cabin dark?'

'Yes, monsieur, since my wife was asleep.'

'The deck as well?'

'Definitely.'

'What happened next?'

'A long time afterwards, I heard the noise of a car engine, as if someone had parked not far from the boat.'

'Did you go and see?'

'No, monsieur. Why would I?'

'Go on.'

'A bit later, there was a splash.'

'As if someone had fallen in the river?'

'Yes, monsieur.'

'What did you do then?'

'I went up the ladder and put my head out through the hatch.'

'What did you see?'

'Two men running to the car.'

'So there was a car?'

'Yes, monsieur. A red car. A Peugeot 403.'

'It was bright enough for you to make it out?'

'There's a street lamp just above the wall.'

'What did the two men look like?'

'The shorter one was broad-shouldered and was wearing a light-coloured raincoat.'

'What about the other one?'

'I didn't see him very well because he was the first to get in the car. He immediately started the engine.'

'Did you see the registration number?'

'The what?'

'The number on the licence plate?'

'I only know there were two 9s and it ended in 75.'

'When did you hear the yelling?'

'When the car got going.'

'In other words, a certain amount of time passed between the moment the man was thrown in the water and the moment he started yelling? Otherwise, you would have heard him earlier?'

'I suppose so, monsieur. It's quieter at night than it is now.'

'What time was this?'

'After midnight.'

'Was there anyone walking on the bridge?'

'I didn't look up.'

Above the wall, where the street ran, a few pedestrians had stopped, intrigued by these men having a discussion on the deck of a barge. It seemed to Maigret that the tramps had moved forwards a few metres. As for the crane, it was still drawing sand from the hold of the *Poitou* and emptying it into the lorries waiting their turn.

'Did he shout loudly?'

'Yes, monsieur.'

'What kind of shout? Was he calling for help?'

'He was yelling. Then there was silence. Then . . .'

'What did you do?'

'I jumped in the lifeboat and untied it.'

'Could you see the drowning man?'

'No, monsieur, not right away. The skipper of the *Poitou* must have heard him, too, because he was running along the deck of his barge trying to grab hold of something with his hook.'

'Carry on.'

Van Houtte was clearly doing the best he could, but it was hard for him, and you could see the sweat form on his forehead.

'"There! There!" he was saying.'

'Who?'

'The skipper of the *Poitou*.'

'And you saw him?'

'At times I could see him, at other times not.'

'Because the body was sinking?'

'Yes, monsieur. And being dragged away by the current.'

'Your lifeboat, too, I suppose?'

'Yes, monsieur. My colleague jumped in.'

'The skipper of the *Poitou*?'

Jef sighed, probably thinking that the people he was talking to were not very clever. As far as he was concerned, it was quite simple, and he must have experienced similar scenes several times in his life.

'The two of you fished him out?'

'Yes.'

'How was he?'

'He still had his eyes open. When we got him in the lifeboat he threw up.'

'Did he say anything?'

'No, monsieur.'

'Did he seem scared?'

'No, monsieur.'

'How did he seem?'

'He didn't seem anything. In the end, he stopped moving, and the water kept coming out of his mouth.'

'Did he still have his eyes open?'

'Yes, monsieur. I thought he was dead.'

'Did you go to fetch help?'

'No, monsieur. Not me.'

'Your colleague from the *Poitou*?'

'No. Someone called to us from the bridge.'

'So there was someone on Pont Marie?

'At that point, yes. He asked us if someone had been in

the water. I said yes. He called out that he was going to inform the police.'

'Did he do that?'

'I suppose so, because a bit later two officers arrived on bicycles.'

'Was it already raining?'

'It started raining and thundering when the man was hoisted on to the deck.'

'The deck of your barge?'

'Yes.'

'Did your wife wake up?'

'There was light in the cabin. Anneke had put a coat on and was looking at us.'

'When did you see the blood?'

'When the man was laid out next to the helm. It was coming out through a crack he had in his head.'

'A crack?'

'A hole. I don't know what you call it.'

'Did the police arrive immediately?'

'Almost immediately.'

'And what about the passer-by who informed them?'

'I didn't see him again.'

'Do you know who he is?'

'No, monsieur.'

In the morning light, it took something of an effort to imagine that nocturnal scene, which Jef Van Houtte was recounting as best he could, searching for his words as if having to translate them one by one from Flemish.

'I assume you know that the tramp was hit on the head before being thrown in the water?'

'That's what the doctor said. One of the policemen had gone to fetch a doctor. Then an ambulance came. Once the wounded man had gone, I had to wash the deck, because there was a big pool of blood.'

'What do you think happened?'

'I don't know, monsieur.'

'You told the police officers—'

'I said what I thought, right?'

'Could you repeat it?'

'I assume he was sleeping under the bridge.'

'But you hadn't seen him before?'

'I hadn't paid attention. There are always people sleeping under the bridges.'

'All right. A car came down the ramp . . .'

'A red car. That, I'm sure of.'

'And it stopped not far from your barge?'

He nodded and held out his arm towards a particular point on the quayside.

'Was the engine still running?'

This time, he shook his head.

'But you heard footsteps?'

'Yes, monsieur.'

'The footsteps of two people?'

'I saw two men going back to the car.'

'You didn't see them walk to the bridge?'

'I was below, working on the engine.'

'And you think these two individuals, one of whom was wearing a light-coloured raincoat, hit the tramp while he was sleeping and threw him in the Seine?'

'By the time I got up on deck, he was already in the water.'

'The doctor's report states that he can't have sustained that injury to the head by falling in the water. Not even during an accidental fall from the bank.'

Van Houtte was looking at them as if to say that this was none of his business.

'Can we question your wife?'

'I don't mind you talking to Anneke. But she won't understand you, she only speaks Flemish.'

The deputy prosecutor looked at Maigret as if to ask him if he had any questions, and Maigret shook his head. If he did have any, it would be for later, once these gentlemen from the prosecutor's office had gone.

'When will we be able to leave?' the bargee asked.

'As soon as you've signed your statement. Providing you let us know where you're going.'

'To Rouen.'

'You'll need to keep us informed of your movements after that. My clerk will come and get you to sign the documents.'

'When?'

'Probably early this afternoon.'

That obviously upset the bargee.

'By the way, what time did your brother get back?'

'Just after the ambulance left.'

'Many thanks.'

Jef Van Houtte again helped him across the narrow gangplank, and the little group headed towards the bridge, while the tramps, for their part, moved a few metres back.

'What do you think, Maigret?'

'I think it's strange. Tramps don't usually get attacked.'

Against the stone wall under the arch of Pont Marie, there was something like a den. It was shapeless, it had no name, and yet – for some time now, apparently – it had been the lair of a human being.

The deputy prosecutor's astonishment was amusing to see, and Maigret couldn't help saying to him:

'You find them under all the bridges. There's even a shelter just like this right opposite Quai des Orfèvres.'

'Don't the police do anything?'

'If they're demolished, they reappear a bit further on.'

It was made up of old crates and pieces of tarpaulin. There was just enough room for a man to be able to huddle there. On the ground were straw, torn blankets and newspapers that gave off a strong smell, in spite of the draught.

The deputy prosecutor took care not to touch anything, and it was Maigret who bent down to conduct a rapid inventory.

A cylinder of sheet metal, with holes and a grille, had served as a stove and was still covered in whitish ash. Close by, pieces of charcoal gathered God alone knew where. Shifting the blankets, Maigret exposed what amounted to a kind of treasure: two chunks of stale bread, some ten centimetres of garlic sausage and, in another corner, some books, whose titles he read under his breath.

'*Sagesse* by Verlaine . . . *Oraisons funèbres* by Bossuet . . .'

He picked up a booklet that must have been lying for a long time in the rain and had probably been picked out of a dustbin. It was an old issue of the *Presse médicale*.

Finally, half a book, the second half only: the *Memorial of Saint Helena*.

Dantziger seemed as astonished as the deputy prosecutor.

'Odd reading matter,' he remarked.

'He may not have chosen it himself.'

Also under the torn blankets, Maigret discovered clothes: a much patched and paint-stained grey pullover, which had probably belonged to a painter, a pair of yellow drill trousers, felt slippers with holes in the heels and five odd socks. Finally, a pair of scissors with one of its blades broken.

'Is the man dead?' Deputy Prosecutor Parrain asked, all the while keeping his distance as if afraid of catching fleas.

'He was still alive an hour ago, when I phoned the Hôtel-Dieu.'

'Do they hope to save him?'

'They're trying. He has a fractured skull, and they're also afraid he might develop pneumonia.'

Maigret was fingering a dilapidated pram the tramp must have used when searching through dustbins. Turning to the little group of tramps, who were still watching, he looked at them, one after the other. Some turned away. Others just looked dazed.

'You, come here!' he said to the woman, pointing a finger at her.

If this had happened thirty years earlier, when he was working the beat, he would have been able to put a name to every face: in those days, he knew most of the tramps in Paris.

They hadn't changed much, as a matter of fact, although there were a lot fewer of them.

'Where do you sleep?'

The woman smiled, as if to win him over.

'There,' she said pointing to Pont Louis-Philippe.

'Did you know the man who was fished out of the river last night?'

Her face was puffy, and her breath smelled of sour wine. Her hands on her belly, she nodded.

'We called him Doc.'

'Why?'

'Because he was an educated man. They say he really used to be a doctor.'

'Had he been sleeping rough for a long time?'

'Years.'

'How many?'

'I don't know. I've stopped counting.'

That made her laugh, and she pushed back a grey strand of hair that was falling over her face. With her mouth closed, she looked about sixty, but when she spoke, she revealed an almost entirely toothless jaw and seemed much older. Her eyes, though, were still lively. From time to time, she would turn to the others, as if calling on them to bear witness.

'Isn't that so?' she would ask them.

They nodded, although ill at ease in the presence of the police and these excessively well-dressed gentlemen.

'Did he live alone?'

That made her laugh again.

'Who would he have lived with?'

'Has he always lived under this bridge?'

'Not always. When I first met him he was under Pont Neuf. And, before that, Quai de Bercy.'

'Did he do Les Halles?'

Wasn't it in Les Halles that most tramps gathered at night?

'No,' she replied.

'The dustbins?'

'Sometimes.'

So, despite the pram, he didn't specialize in old papers and cloths, which explained how come he was already asleep so early during the night.

'Mainly, he was a sandwich man.'

'What else do you know about him?'

'Nothing.'

'Didn't he ever talk to you?'

'Of course he did. I even cut his hair for him every now and again. We have to help each other.'

'Did he drink a lot?'

Maigret knew that the question was rather meaningless: they pretty much all drank.

'Red wine?'

'Like everyone else.'

'A lot?'

'I never saw him drunk. He's not like me.'

And she laughed again.

'I know you, you know, and I know you're not nasty. You questioned me once, in your office, a long time ago, maybe twenty years ago, when I was still working around Porte Saint-Denis.'

'Did you hear anything last night?'

She pointed to Pont Louis-Philippe, as if to demonstrate the distance between it and Pont Marie.

'It's too far.'

'So you didn't see anything?'

'Only the lights of the ambulance. I went a bit closer, not too close – I was scared they'd haul me in – and I realized that it was an ambulance.'

'What about you three?' Maigret asked, turning to the male tramps.

They shook their heads, still nervous.

'Shall we go and see the skipper of the *Poitou*?' the deputy prosecutor suggested, ill at ease in these surroundings.

The man was waiting for them. He was quite different from Van Houtte. He, too, had his wife and children on board, but the barge didn't belong to him and it almost always made the same journey, from the sandpits of the Haute-Seine to Paris. His name was Justin Goulet, and he was forty-five years old, short-legged, with cunning eyes. An extinguished cigarette hung from his lips.

Here, they had to speak loudly, because of the noise of the crane, which was still unloading sand very close to them.

'It's funny, isn't it?'

'What is?'

'That people should take the trouble to knock out a tramp and throw him in the river.'

'Did you see them?'

'I didn't see anything at all.'

'Where were you?'

'When they hit the man? In my bed.'

'What did you hear?'

'I heard someone yelling.'

'No car?'

'I may have heard a car, but there are always cars driving by up there, and I didn't pay attention.'

'Did you go up on deck?'

'Yes, in my pyjamas. I didn't bother to put on trousers.'

'What about your wife?'

'She was half asleep. She asked me where I was going.'

'Once you were up on deck, what did you see?'

'Nothing. The Seine was swirling about, as always. I called out, "Ahoy there!" hoping he'd answer so I could know which side he was.'

'Where was Jef Van Houtte at this time?'

'The Flemish fellow? I eventually saw him on the deck of his barge. He started untying his lifeboat. When he came level with me, thanks to the current, I jumped in. The other man was still in the water. He'd come to the surface from time to time then disappear again. The Flemish fellow tried to grab him with my gaff.'

'A pole ending in a big iron hook?'

'Like all gaffs.'

'Could he have been hit on the head when you were trying to hook him?'

'Definitely not. We actually caught him by the hem of his trousers. I immediately leaned over and grabbed his leg.'

'Was he unconscious?'

'His eyes were open.'

'Did he say anything?'

'He was throwing up water. Once we got him on the Flemish barge, we noticed he was bleeding.'

'That's everything, I think, isn't it?' asked the deputy

prosecutor, who didn't seem especially interested in this story.

'I'll take care of the rest,' Maigret replied.

'Are you going to the hospital?'

'I'll go later. According to the doctors, it'll be hours before he's able to talk.'

'Keep me informed.'

'I'll be sure to.'

As they again passed under Pont Marie, Maigret said to Lapointe:

'Phone the local police station and ask them to send me an officer.'

'Where shall I find you, chief?'

'Here.'

He solemnly shook hands with the people from the prosecutor's office.

2.

'Are they judges?' the fat woman asked, watching the three men walk away.

'Magistrates,' Maigret corrected her.

'Isn't that the same thing?' She gave a short whistle. 'They're making as much fuss as if he's someone important! Does that mean he was a real doctor?'

Maigret had no idea. He didn't seem in any great hurry to find out. He was living in the present, still with the sense of things he had lived through a long time before. Lapointe had disappeared at the top of the ramp. The deputy prosecutor, flanked by the examining magistrate and the clerk of the court, was looking where he was walking, for fear of dirtying his shoes.

Black and white in the sun, the *Zwarte Zwaan* was as clean on the outside as its kitchen must be. Van Houtte was standing near the helm, looking in Maigret's direction. A slight, childlike woman with blonde hair that was almost white was bending over the baby's cradle, changing her nappy.

There was the constant noise of cars passing along Quai des Célestins, as well as the noise of the crane unloading sand from the *Poitou*. Neither drowned out the singing of birds or the lapping of the water.

The three tramps continued to keep their distance, and

only the fat woman followed Maigret under the bridge. Her blouse, which must once have been red, had turned candy-pink.

'What's your name?'

'Léa. They call me Fat Léa.'

That made her laugh and shook her huge breasts.

'Where were you last night?'

'I told you.'

'Was there anyone with you?'

'Only Dédé, the shortest one over there, the one with his back to us.'

'Is he your friend?'

'They're all my friends.'

'Do you always sleep under the same bridge?'

'I move sometimes . . . What are you looking for?'

Maigret had again bent over the disparate objects that constituted Doc's belongings. He felt more at ease now that the magistrates had left. He was taking his time, discovering, beneath the rags, a frying pan, a mess tin, a spoon and a fork.

Then he tried on a pair of steel-rimmed glasses with one cracked lens, and everything became blurred in front of his eyes.

'He only used them for reading,' Fat Léa said.

'What surprises me,' he began, looking at her insistently, 'is not finding . . .'

Not letting him finish, she moved some two metres away and produced a still half-full litre bottle of purplish-blue wine from behind a large stone.

'Have you been drinking it?'

'Yes. I was planning to have the rest. It'll have gone off anyway by the time Doc comes back.'

'When did you take it?'

'Last night, after the ambulance took him away.'

'Have you touched anything else?'

With a serious expression on her face, she spat on the ground.

'No, I swear!'

He believed her. He knew from experience that tramps don't steal from each other. In fact, they rarely steal anything at all, not only because they would immediately be caught, but because of a kind of indifference.

Opposite, on Ile Saint-Louis, the windows of cosy apartments stood open. A woman could be seen brushing her hair at her dressing table.

'Do you know where he bought his wine?'

'I saw him coming out of a bistro in Rue de l'Ave-Maria a few times. It's quite near here, on the corner of Rue des Jardins.'

'How was Doc with the others?'

Trying to please him, she thought this over.

'I don't know. He wasn't all that different.'

'Did he ever talk about his life?'

'Nobody does. Unless they're very drunk.'

'Was he ever drunk?'

'Not really.'

From the pile of old newspapers the tramp had used to keep warm, Maigret had just taken out a little painted wooden horse with one leg broken. He wasn't surprised. Nor was Fat Léa.

Someone in espadrilles had just come down the ramp, silently and with a spring in his step, and was approaching the Belgian barge, holding in each hand a string bag full of provisions from which two big loaves of bread and a few leeks stuck out.

It was the brother, there was no doubt about it, because he looked like Jef Van Houtte, only younger, with less pronounced features. He was wearing blue cotton trousers and a sweater with white stripes. Once on the boat, he spoke to Jef, then looked in Maigret's direction.

'Don't touch anything. I may need you again. If you find out anything . . .'

'Can you see me coming to your office, looking like this?'

That made her laugh once again. Pointing to the bottle, she asked:

'Can I finish it?'

He nodded and went to meet Lapointe, who was just returning, accompanied by a uniformed officer. He gave the latter instructions to guard the pile of things that constituted Doc's entire fortune until a technician from Criminal Records arrived.

After which, with Lapointe by his side, he walked over to the *Zwarte Zwaan*.

'Are you Hubert Van Houtte?'

More taciturn or more suspicious than his brother, Hubert merely nodded.

'Did you go dancing last night?'

'Is there anything wrong with that?'

He didn't have such a strong accent. Maigret and Lapointe, still standing on the quayside, had to look up at him.

'Which dance hall did you go to?'

'It was near Place de la Bastille, in a narrow street where there are half a dozen of them. This one's called Léon's.'

'Did you already know it?'

'I've been several times.'

'So you don't know what happened?'

'Only what my brother told me.'

Smoke was emerging from a copper chimney on deck. The woman and the child had gone down into the cabin, and from where they stood Maigret and Lapointe could smell cooking.

'When will we be able to leave?'

'Probably this afternoon. As soon as the magistrate has got your brother to sign his statement.'

Hubert Van Houtte was clean and well groomed, with the same pink complexion and very fair hair.

Soon afterwards, Maigret and Lapointe crossed Quai des Célestins and found a bistro called the Petit Turin on the corner of Rue de l'Ave-Maria. The owner was standing in the doorway in his shirtsleeves. There was nobody inside.

'Can we come in?'

He stood aside, surprised to see people like them enter his establishment, which was tiny and had only three tables for customers, in addition to the counter. The walls were painted apple green. From the ceiling hung sausages, cured meats and strange yellow cheeses shaped like overfilled goatskins.

'What can I get you?'

'Wine.'

'Chianti?'

Straw-covered bottles filled one shelf, but it was from a bottle taken from under the counter that the owner filled the glasses, watching the two men curiously.

'Do you know a tramp nicknamed Doc?'

'How is he? I hope he's not dead?'

They had gone from a Flemish accent to an Italian one, from the calm demeanour of Jef Van Houtte and his brother Hubert to the bar owner's demonstrative gestures.

'So you know about it?' Maigret asked.

'I know something happened last night.'

'Who told you?'

'Another tramp, this morning.'

'What exactly did he tell you?'

'That there was a commotion near Pont Marie, and that an ambulance came for Doc.'

'Is that all?'

'Apparently some bargees took him out of the water.'

'Is this where Doc bought his wine?'

'Yes, quite often.'

'Did he drink a lot?'

'About two litres a day. When he had money.'

'How did he earn money?'

'The way they all do. By helping out at Les Halles or in other places. Or else walking with sandwich boards in the street. I was happy to give him credit.'

'Why?'

'Because he wasn't like the other tramps. He saved my wife.'

They could see her in the kitchen, almost as fat as Léa, but very alert.

'Are you talking about me?'

'I'm telling them how Doc . . .'

She came into the bistro, wiping her hands on her apron.

'Is it true they tried to kill him? Are you from the police? Do you think he'll pull through?'

'We don't know yet,' Maigret replied evasively. 'In what way did he save you?'

'Well, if you'd seen me only two years ago, you wouldn't recognize me now. I was covered in eczema, and my face was as red as a piece of meat on a butcher's slab. It had been going on for months and months. At the clinic, they suggested all kinds of treatments, they gave me ointments that smelled so bad I couldn't stand myself. Nothing worked . . . I was pretty much forbidden to eat, not that I had any appetite. They also gave me injections.'

The owner was listening and nodding.

'One day, when Doc was sitting right over there, in the corner, near the door, and I was complaining to the vegetable seller, I could feel him looking at me in a funny way. A bit later, he told me in the same voice as he would have ordered a glass of wine, "I think I can cure you." I asked him if he really was a doctor, and he smiled and said, "They haven't taken away my right to practise."'

'Did he give you a prescription?'

'No. He asked me for a bit of money, two hundred francs, if I remember correctly, and went himself to the pharmacy to get some little powder tablets. "Take one in warm water before every meal," he said, "and wash with very salty water, morning and evening." Believe it or not, two months later my skin was back to the way it is now.'

'Did he treat anyone else apart from you?'

'I don't know. He didn't talk a lot.'

'Did he come here every day?'

'Almost every day, to buy his two litres.'

'Was he always alone? Did you ever see him with anyone you didn't know?'

'No.'

'Did he ever tell you his real name, or where he used to live?'

'I know only that he had a daughter. We have one ourselves, she's at school right now. Once, when he was looking at her in an odd kind of way, he said, "Don't worry. I had a little girl, too."'

Was Lapointe surprised to see Maigret attach so much importance to this story of a tramp? In the newspapers, it would be a minor item of just a few lines at most.

What Lapointe didn't know, because he was too young, was that this was the first time in Maigret's career that a crime had been committed against a tramp.

'How much do I owe you?'

'Won't you have another? To the health of poor Doc?'

They drank the second glass, which the Italian refused to let them pay for. Then they crossed Pont Marie. A few minutes later, they entered Hôtel-Dieu hospital through the grey archway. There, they had to negotiate for a long time with a surly woman barricaded behind a counter.

'Don't you know his name?'

'All I know is that on the riverbank he's known as Doc and he was brought here last night.'

'I wasn't here last night. Which department did they take him to?'

'I have no idea. I spoke to an intern earlier on the phone. He didn't mention an operation . . .'

'Do you know the name of the intern?'

'No.'

She kept turning the pages of a register and made a few telephone calls.

'What's your name again?'

'Detective Chief Inspector Maigret.'

That meant nothing to this woman, who repeated into the phone:

'Detective Chief Inspector Maigret.'

At last, after some ten minutes, she sighed, as if doing them a favour:

'Take staircase C to the third floor. You'll find the head nurse of the department.'

They passed male nurses, younger doctors and patients in hospital garb and glimpsed rows of beds through open doors.

On the third floor, they had to wait some more because the head nurse was having an animated conversation with two men and seemed to be refusing what they were asking of her.

'I can't do anything about it,' she finally said. 'Talk to the management. I don't make the rules.'

They walked away, muttering angrily to themselves, and she turned to Maigret.

'Are you the ones here for the tramp?'

'Detective Chief Inspector Maigret,' he repeated.

She searched in her memory. The name didn't mean anything to her either. They were in another world, a world of numbered rooms, compartmentalized departments, vast wards lined with beds, with a sheet of paper covered in mysterious signs hanging at the foot of each one.

'How is he?'

'I think Professor Magnin is dealing with him at the moment.'

'Has he been operated on?'

'Who mentioned an operation?'

'I don't know. I thought . . .'

Maigret felt out of place here and became hesitant.

'What name did you admit him under?'

'The name that was on his identity card.'

'Do you have the card?'

'I can show it to you.'

She went into a little glass-walled office at the end of the corridor and immediately found a grimy identity card still damp with water from the Seine.

Surname: Keller.
Christian names: François Marie Florentin.
Profession: Ragman.
Born: Mulhouse, Bas-Rhin.

According to this document, the man was sixty-three, and his address in Paris was a rooming house on Place

Maubert, which Maigret knew well and which was used as an official abode by a number of tramps.

'Has he regained consciousness?'

She tried to take back the identity card, but Maigret slipped it into his pocket.

'That's not allowed,' she grumbled. 'The regulations—'

'Is Keller in a private room?'

'What now?'

'Take me to him.'

She hesitated and finally gave in.

'All right, you can sort it out with the professor.'

Preceding them, she opened the third door, behind which were two rows of beds, all occupied. Most of the patients lay there, their eyes open; two or three at the far end, in hospital garb, stood chatting in low voices.

Near one of the beds, towards the middle of the ward, some ten young men and women in white coats, with caps on their heads, stood around a smaller, stocky man with crew-cut hair, also dressed in white, who was apparently giving them a lesson.

'You can't disturb him for the moment. You can see he's busy.'

All the same, she went and whispered a few words in the professor's ear, and the professor threw a distant glance at Maigret and resumed the course of his explanations.

'He'll be finished in a few minutes. He asks you to wait in his office.'

She took them there. It wasn't a large room, and there were only two chairs. On the desk, in a silver frame, a photograph of a woman and three children, their heads touching.

After some hesitation, Maigret emptied his pipe in the ashtray, which was full of cigarette ends, and filled another.

'Sorry to have kept you waiting, inspector. When my nurse told me who you were, I was a little surprised. After all . . .'

Was he about to say that after all they were only dealing with a tramp? No.

'. . . this is quite a trivial case, is it not?'

'I know almost nothing about it yet. I'm counting on you to enlighten me.'

'A fracture of the skull, quite clean, fortunately, as my assistant must have told you on the phone this morning.'

'He hadn't yet been X-rayed . . .'

'That's been done now . . . He has a good chance of pulling through, because the brain doesn't seem to be affected.'

'Could the fracture have been caused by a fall from the riverbank?'

'Definitely not . . . The man received a violent blow with a heavy instrument, a hammer, a spanner, perhaps a tyre lever.'

'And that made him lose consciousness?'

'Yes, to the extent that he's now in a coma and may stay in it for several days . . . Just as he may come round any hour now.'

Maigret remembered the riverbank, Doc's shelter, the

muddy water flowing by a few metres away and Jef Van Houtte's words.

'I'm sorry to insist . . . You say he received a blow on the head . . . Just one?'

'Why do you ask me that?'

'It may be important.'

'At first glance, I thought he might have received several blows.'

'Why?'

'Because one ear is torn, and there are several wounds, shallow ones, on the face . . . But now that he's been shaved, I've been able to examine him closely . . .'

'And your conclusion is . . . ?'

'Where did it happen?'

'Under Pont Marie.'

'In a fight?'

'Apparently not. It seems the man was lying there asleep when he was attacked . . . According to your observations, is that plausible?'

'Perfectly plausible.'

'And you think he immediately lost consciousness?'

'I'm pretty much certain of it. And from what you've just told me, I understand the torn ear and the scratches on the face. He was found in the Seine, wasn't he? Those secondary wounds indicate that instead of being carried he was dragged to the river across the cobbles. Is there sand on the riverbank?'

'A sand barge is being unloaded a few metres away.'

'I found some in the wounds.'

'So in your opinion, this man, this Doc—'

'I beg your pardon?' the professor said in surprise.

'That's his nickname on the riverbank. He may really have been a doctor once.'

Which would also make him the first doctor in thirty years whom Maigret had encountered sleeping rough by the Seine, although he had once come across a former chemistry teacher from a provincial high school and, a few years later, a woman who had had her hour of fame as a bareback rider in a circus.

'I'm convinced he was lying down, probably asleep, when his assailant or assailants hit him.'

'Just one, since there was only one blow.'

'Precisely. He lost consciousness, so they may have thought he was dead.'

'Perfectly plausible.'

'Instead of carrying him, they dragged him to the edge of the riverbank and tipped him into the water.'

The professor was listening gravely, thoughtfully.

'Does that hold up?' Maigret insisted.

'Totally.'

'Is it medically possible that, once in the river, while the current was sweeping him away, he started crying out?'

The professor scratched his head.

'You're asking a lot of me, and I wouldn't like to answer you too categorically . . . Let's say it's not impossible. It could have been the shock of the cold water.'

'You mean he might have regained consciousness?'

'Not necessarily. Patients in a coma speak and move. It's a possibility.'

'Did he say anything while you were examining him?'

'He moaned several times.'

'Apparently when he was taken out of the water, his eyes were open.'

'That doesn't mean anything . . . I assume you'd like to see him? Come with me.'

He led them to the third floor. The head nurse watched them with some astonishment and doubtless also a hint of disapproval.

The patients in the beds followed the little group with their eyes until it stopped beside one of them.

'You can't see much.'

Indeed, the tramp's head and face were wrapped in bandages, leaving only the eyes, nostrils and mouth uncovered.

'What's the likelihood he'll pull through?'

'Seventy per cent. Let's say eighty, given how strong the heart still is.'

'Many thanks.'

'You'll be informed as soon as he regains consciousness. Leave your telephone number with the head nurse.'

It felt good to be outside again, to see the sun, the passers-by, a yellow and red coach disgorging its tourists on to the square in front of Notre-Dame.

Maigret again walked without saying anything, his hands behind his back, and Lapointe, sensing that he was preoccupied, avoided speaking.

They went in through the entrance of the Police Judiciaire, climbed the grand staircase, made to seem all the dustier by the sunlight, and at last entered Maigret's office.

Maigret began by flinging the window wide open and watching a line of barges travelling downstream.

'We have to send someone from upstairs to examine his things.'

'Upstairs' meant Criminal Records, with its technicians and specialists.

'The best thing would be to take the van and move everything.'

He wasn't afraid the other tramps would grab the various objects belonging to Doc, he was more afraid of scavenging children.

'As for you, I'd like you to go to the Highways Department. There can't be all that many red Peugeot 403s in Paris. Make a note of the numbers with two 9s. Get help from as many men as it'll take to check with the owners.'

'Got it, chief.'

Once alone, Maigret arranged his pipes and went through the memos piled up on his desk. Because of the fine weather, he considered having lunch at the Brasserie Dauphine, but decided in the end to go home.

At this hour, the dining room was filled with sunlight. Madame Maigret was wearing a flowery pink dress that reminded him of Fat Léa's blouse, which was almost the same pink.

He was eating his calves' liver *en papillotes*, lost in thought, when his wife asked him:

'What are you thinking about?'

'My tramp.'

'What tramp?'

'A fellow who may once have been a doctor.'

'What has he done?'

'Nothing as far as I know. He got his head cracked open as he was sleeping under Pont Marie, after which he was thrown in the river.'

'Is he dead?'

'Some bargees fished him out in time.'

'Why would anyone have wanted to harm him?'

'That's what I'm wondering. By the way, he's from your brother-in-law's neck of the woods.'

Madame Maigret's sister lived in Mulhouse with her husband, who was an engineer for the Highways Department. The Maigrets had often been to visit them.

'What's his name?'

'Keller. François Keller.'

'It's odd, but the name sounds familiar.'

'It's quite a common name in that area.'

'How about if I phoned my sister?'

He shrugged. Why not? He didn't believe it would lead anywhere, but it would please his wife.

As soon as she had served the coffee, she called Mulhouse and only had to wait a few minutes to be put through, during which time she kept repeating softly, like someone trying to summon a memory:

'Keller . . . François Keller . . .'

The phone rang.

'Hello? . . . Yes, mademoiselle, I'm the one asking for Mulhouse . . . Is that you, Florence? . . . What? . . . It's me, yes . . . No, nothing's wrong . . . From Paris. I'm at home . . . He's right here, drinking his coffee . . . He's fine. Everything's fine . . . Here, too. It's spring at last. How are the children? . . . The flu? I had it last week . . . No, it wasn't serious . . . Listen, that's not why I'm calling. Do you by any chance remember a man named Keller? . . . François Keller . . . What? . . . I'll ask him . . .'

Turning to Maigret, she asked:

'How old is he?'

'Sixty-four.'

'Sixty-four . . . Yes . . . Did you know him personally? . . . What's that? . . . Don't cut us off, mademoiselle . . . Hello? . . . Yes, he was a doctor . . . For the last half hour, I've been trying to remember who I heard it from . . . Do you think it was your husband? . . . Yes . . . Wait, I'll tell mine what you told me, he looks as if he's getting impatient . . . He married a Merville girl. Who are the Mervilles? . . . A court counsellor? . . . He married the daughter of a court counsellor? . . . Right . . . He died . . . A long time ago . . . Right . . . Don't be surprised if I repeat it all, otherwise I'd be afraid of forgetting something . . . An old Mulhouse family . . . The grandfather was a mayor and . . . I can't hear well . . . His statue . . . No, I don't think it's important. It doesn't matter if you're not sure . . . Hello? . . . Keller married her . . . The only daughter . . . Rue du Sauvage? . . . The couple lived in Rue du Sauvage . . . An eccentric? . . . Why? . . . You're not exactly sure . . . Oh, yes, I understand! Uncivilized, you mean, a savage, like the street.'

She looked at Maigret as if to say that she was doing her best.

'Yes . . . Yes . . . It doesn't matter if it's not interesting. With him, you never know. Sometimes, an unimportant detail . . . Yes . . . What year? . . . So that was about twenty years ago . . . She inherited money from an aunt, and he left . . . Oh, not right away . . . He lived with her for another year . . . Did they have children? . . . A daughter? . . . Who to? . . . Rousselet, of the pharmaceutical company? . . . Does she live in Paris?'

She repeated for her husband:

'They had a daughter who married the son of the Rousselet family, the pharmaceutical people, and they live in Paris . . .'

And, turning back to the telephone:

'I understand . . . Listen. See if you can find out any more . . . Yes . . . Thank you . . . Kiss your husband and children for me. Call me back any time. I'm not going out.'

The sound of kisses. Once again, she addressed Maigret.

'I was sure I knew the name. Did you get all that? Apparently it really is that Keller, François, who was a doctor and married the daughter of a magistrate who died just before the wedding.'

'What about the mother?' he asked.

She looked at him sharply, wondering if he was being ironic.

'I don't know, Florence didn't tell me . . . About twenty years ago, Madame Keller inherited money from an aunt of hers, and now she's very rich . . . The doctor was an eccentric. Did you hear what I said on the phone? A savage, my sister called him. They left their house and moved into a mansion near the cathedral. He spent another year with her, then suddenly disappeared. Florence is going to phone her friends, especially the older ones, to see if she can get any more information. She's promised to call me back. Is this of interest?'

'Everything's of interest,' he sighed, getting up from his armchair and going to the rack to change pipes.

'Do you think you'll have to go to Mulhouse?'

'I don't know yet.'

'Would you take me?'

They both smiled. The window was open. They were bathed in sunlight, and their minds turned towards holidays.

'See you this evening. I'll make a note of everything she tells me. Even if you're going to laugh at the two of us.'

3.

Young Lapointe had to go all over Paris in search of the red Peugeot 403s. Janvier wasn't in his place in the inspectors' office either because he had been called to the clinic, where he was pacing the corridors, waiting for his wife to give birth to their fourth child.

'Are you doing anything urgent, Lucas?'

'It can wait, chief.'

'Come into my office for a moment.'

It was in order to send him to the Hôtel-Dieu to find Doc's effects. He hadn't thought of it in the morning.

'They'll probably send you from office to office and bring up all kinds of bureaucratic objections. You'd better take along a letter that impresses them, with as many seals as possible.'

'Who shall I get it signed by?'

'Sign it yourself. With them, it's the seals that count. I'd also like to have this François Keller's fingerprints ... Actually, it'd be easier to get me the hospital's director on the phone.'

From the window-sill, a sparrow was watching the two of them move about in what must to its eyes be a nest of men. Very politely, Maigret announced Sergeant Lucas' visit, and everything went very well.

'You don't need a letter,' he announced, hanging up.

'They'll take you straight to the director, and he'll show you around himself.'

Once he was alone, he leafed through the Paris telephone directory.

'Rousselet . . . Rousselet . . . Amédée . . . Arthur . . . Aline . . .'

There were lots of Rousselets, but there, in bolder letters, were the words *René Rousselet Laboratories*.

The labs were in the fourteenth arrondissement, near Porte d'Orléans. The private address of this particular Rousselet was just below it: Boulevard Suchet, in the sixteenth.

It was 2.30. The weather was just as radiant as before, after a gust of wind that had raised the dust from the pavements and made a storm look briefly possible.

'Hello? I'd like to speak to Madame Rousselet, please.'

'Who shall I say is calling?' a deep, very pleasant woman's voice asked.

'Detective Chief Inspector Maigret, Police Judiciaire.'

There was a silence, then:

'Can you tell me what it's about?'

'It's personal.'

'I'm Madame Rousselet.'

'You were born in Mulhouse, and your maiden name is Keller, is that correct?'

'Yes.'

'I'd like to have a conversation with you as soon as possible. May I come to see you at home?'

'Do you have bad news to tell me?'

'I just need some information.'

'When would you like to come?'

'As soon as I can get to you.'

He heard her say to someone, presumably a child:

'Let me speak, Jeannot.'

She sounded surprised, intrigued, anxious.

'I'll be waiting, inspector. Our apartment is on the third floor.'

That morning, he had loved the atmosphere of the riverbank, which had aroused so many memories, in particular so many strolls with Madame Maigret, when they would walk along the Seine from one end of Paris to the other. Now he was just as appreciative of the quiet avenues, the trees, the opulent houses of the affluent neighbourhood where he was taken in a little police car driven by Inspector Torrence.

'Shall I go up with you, chief?'

'I think it's best if you don't.'

The building had a wrought-iron door lined with glass, the entrance hall was of white marble, and the spacious lift rose in silence, without any jolting or squeaking. He barely had time to press the doorbell when the door opened, and a manservant in a white jacket took his hat.

'This way, please.'

There was a red ball in the hall, a doll on the carpet. He glimpsed a nurse pushing a little girl in white towards the far end of a corridor. Another door opened, revealing a boudoir just off the main drawing room.

'Come in, inspector.'

Maigret had calculated that she must be about thirty-five.

She didn't look it. She had brown hair and was dressed in a light tailored suit. Her eyes, as gentle and mellow as her voice, were already questioning him as the manservant closed the door.

'Please sit down. Ever since you phoned me, I've been wondering . . .'

Instead of getting to the point, he asked automatically:

'Do you have several children?'

'Four. The oldest one's eleven, the others are nine, seven and three.'

This was almost certainly the first time a police officer had been in her apartment, and she kept her eyes fixed on him.

'The first thing I wondered was whether something had happened to my husband.'

'Is he in Paris?'

'Not right now. He's attending a conference in Brussels, and I phoned him immediately.'

'How well do you remember your father, Madame Rousselet?'

She seemed to relax very slightly. There were flowers everywhere, and the trees of the Bois de Boulogne could be seen through the tall windows.

'Quite well. Although . . .'

She seemed reluctant to continue.

'When did you last see him?'

'Oh, a long time ago. I was thirteen.'

'Were you still living in Mulhouse?'

'Yes. I didn't come to Paris until after I married.'

'Did you meet your husband in Mulhouse?'

'No, in La Baule, where my mother and I went every year.'

There came the sound of children's voices, cries, something sliding in the corridors.

'Excuse me for a moment.'

She closed the door behind her and spoke in a low but firm voice.

'Please forgive me. They aren't at school today, and I promised I'd take them out.'

'Would you recognize your father?'

'I suppose so . . . Yes.'

He took out Doc's identity card. The photograph, according to the card's date of issue, was about five years old. It was one of those photos taken by an automatic camera, the kind found in department stores, railway stations and even at the Préfecture.

François Keller hadn't shaved for the occasion and had made no effort to clean himself up. His cheeks were overrun with two or three centimetres of beard, which he probably cut with scissors every now and again. His temples were starting to go bald, and his gaze was neutral, indifferent.

'Is this him?'

Holding the card in a hand that shook a little, she leaned forwards to get a better look. She must have been short-sighted.

'It isn't the way I remember him, but I'm pretty sure it's him.'

She leaned even more.

'Perhaps with a magnifying glass . . . Wait, I'll go and get one.'

Placing the identity card on a pedestal table, she left the room and came back a few minutes later with a magnifying glass.

'He had a scar, a small but deep one, above his left eye . . . There it is. You can't see it very well in this picture, but I think it's there . . . Look for yourself.'

He, too, looked through the magnifying glass.

'The reason I remember it is that it's because of me that he hurt himself. We were out for a walk in the country, one Sunday. It was very hot. All along the edge of a cornfield there was a mass of poppies. I wanted to go and pick some. The field was surrounded by barbed wire. I was about eight. My father moved the barbed wire to let me through. He was holding the bottom wire down with his foot and leaning forwards . . . It's funny how well I remember the scene, even though I've forgotten so many other things . . . His foot must have slipped, and the barbed wire suddenly sprang back and hit him in the face. My mother was afraid it had caught his eye. He was bleeding a lot. We walked to a farm to find water and something to make a bandage. He was left with a scar.'

As she spoke, she continued to look anxiously at Maigret, as if delaying the moment when he would tell her the precise reason for his visit.

'Has something happened to him?'

'He was injured last night, in the head again as it happens, but the doctors don't think his life is in any danger.'

'Did it happen in Paris?'

'Yes. On the banks of the Seine. Whoever attacked him then threw him in the river.'

He hadn't taken his eyes off her, watching out for her reactions, and she made no attempt to evade this examination.

'Do you know how your father has been living?'

'Not exactly.'

'What do you mean?'

'When he left us . . .'

'You were thirteen, you said. Do you remember his leaving?'

'No. One morning, I didn't see him in the house, and when I said I was surprised, my mother told me he'd gone on a long journey.'

'When did you find out where he was?'

'A few months later, my mother told me he was in Africa, in the middle of nowhere, treating the natives.'

'Was it true?'

'I suppose it was. In fact, later, people who'd met him there told us about him. He was living in Gabon, in a place hundreds of kilometres from Libreville.'

'Did he stay there long?'

'Several years at least. Some people in Mulhouse considered him a kind of saint. Others . . .'

He was waiting. She hesitated.

'Others called him a hothead, said he was half mad.'

'What about your mother?'

'I think mother had already resigned herself once and for all.'

'How old is she now?'

'Fifty-four. No, fifty-five . . . I know now that he'd left her a letter, which she's never shown me, telling her he would probably never come back and that he was prepared to make things easy for her if she wanted a divorce.'

'Did she get a divorce?'

'No. Mother's a devout Catholic.'

'Does your husband know about all this?'

'Of course. We didn't hide anything from him.'

'Did you know your father was back in Paris?'

She blinked rapidly and almost lied, Maigret was sure of it.

'Yes and no. I've never seen him myself. Mother and I were never completely sure. But someone from Mulhouse told her about a sandwich man he'd seen on Boulevard Saint-Michel who looked very much like my father. This person is an old friend of Mother's. Apparently, when he said the name François, the man jumped but then pretended he hadn't recognized him.'

'Didn't it occur to you or your mother to go to the police?'

'What would be the point? He chose his life. I don't suppose he was cut out to live with us.'

'Didn't you ever wonder about him?'

'I talked about him several times with my husband.'

'And with your mother?'

'I asked her questions, obviously, before and after I married.'

'What's her point of view?'

'It's hard to sum it up, really. She feels sorry for him. So do I. Although I sometimes wonder if he isn't happier this way.'

In a lower voice, with some embarrassment, she added:

'There are people who can't adapt to the kind of life we lead. And then, Mother . . .'

Nervously, she stood up, walked over to the window and looked outside for a moment before turning to face him again.

'I don't have anything bad to say about her. She has her way of looking at things. I suppose we all do. The word "domineering" is too strong, but all the same she likes things to be the way she wants them.'

'After your father left, did you get on well with her?'

'Well enough. All the same, I was pleased to get married and . . .'

'And escape her domination?'

'That's partly it.' She smiled. 'It's not very original. There are lots of young girls who are in the same boat. My mother likes going out, receiving visitors, meeting important people. In Mulhouse, it was in her house that everyone who mattered in town gathered.'

'Even when your father was there?'

'The last two years, yes.'

'Why the last two?'

He remembered Madame Maigret's long telephone conversation with her sister and felt a little upset that he was going to learn more here than his wife was likely to.

'Because mother inherited money from her aunt. Before, we lived quite poorly, in a modest house. We didn't even live in a nice neighbourhood, and my father's patients were mainly workers. Nobody had been expecting that inheritance. We moved house. Mother bought a mansion near the cathedral and she was quite pleased that there was a carved coat of arms above the front door.'

'Did you know your father's family?'

'No. I'd only ever seen his brother a few times before he was killed in the war, in Syria, unless I'm mistaken, not in France anyway.'

'What about his father and mother?'

Once again, there came the sound of children's voices, but she took no notice.

'His mother died of cancer when my father was about fifteen. His father had a carpentry business. According to Mother, he had a dozen people working for him. One fine morning, when my father was still at university, he was found hanging in the workshop, and it emerged that he was about to go bankrupt.'

'But your father still managed to finish his studies?'

'By working in a pharmacy.'

'What was he like?'

'Very gentle . . . I know that's not much of an answer to your question, but it's the main impression I've kept of him. Very gentle and a little sad . . .'

'Did he and your mother quarrel?'

'I never heard him raise his voice. Admittedly, when he wasn't in his surgery, he spent most of his time visiting his patients. I remember my mother telling him off for not taking any care of his appearance, always wearing the same suit that hadn't been ironed, sometimes going for three days without shaving. I used to tell him that he tickled me with his beard when he kissed me.'

'I don't suppose you know anything about your father's relations with his colleagues?'

'What I know, I know through Mother. Only, with her, it's hard to tell what's true from what's more or less true. Not that she lies. She arranges the truth to make it the way she'd like it to be. Seeing that she'd married my father, he had to be someone extraordinary. Your father's the best doctor in the city, she would tell me, probably one of the best in the whole of France. Unfortunately . . .'

She was smiling again.

'You can guess the rest. He couldn't adapt. He refused to be like everyone else. She implied that the reason my grandfather hanged himself wasn't because of his impending bankruptcy but because he suffered from depression. He had a daughter who spent some time in an asylum.'

'What became of her?'

'I don't know. I don't think my mother knows either. In any case, she left Mulhouse.'

'Does your mother still live there?'

'She's been in Paris for a long time now.'

'Could you let me have her address?'

'29b Quai d'Orléans.'

Maigret had given a start, but she didn't notice.

'It's on Ile Saint-Louis. Since the island became one of the most sought-after places in Paris—'

'Do you know where your father was assaulted last night?'

'Of course not.'

'Under Pont Marie. Three hundred metres from where your mother lives.'

She frowned anxiously. 'That's on the other branch of the Seine, isn't it? Mother's windows face Quai de la Tournelle.'

'Does she have a dog?'

'Why do you ask that?'

During the few months that Maigret had lived on Place des Vosges, while they were renovating the building on Boulevard Richard-Lenoir, he and his wife had often gone for an evening stroll around Ile Saint-Louis. That was the time of day when dog owners walked their pets along the riverbank, or got their servants to walk them.

'Mother only keeps birds. She hates dogs and cats.' She changed the subject. 'Where has my father been taken?'

'To the nearest hospital, the Hôtel-Dieu.'

'I suppose you'd like me to—'

'Not now. I may ask you to come and identify him, in order to be absolutely certain as to his identity, but for the moment his head and face are covered in bandages.'

'Is he in a lot of pain?'

'He's in a coma and isn't aware of anything.'

'Why would anyone do that to him?'

'That's what I'm trying to find out.'

'Was there a fight?'

'No. In all likelihood, he was asleep when he was assaulted.'

'Under the bridge?'

He stood up in his turn.

'I assume you're going to see my mother?'

'It's difficult for me to do otherwise.'

'Do you mind if I phone and tell her the news?'

He hesitated. He would have preferred to observe Madame Keller's reactions, but he didn't insist.

'Many thanks, inspector. Will it be in the newspapers?'

'There's probably already a small item about the assault by now, but your father's name certainly won't be in it. I didn't discover it myself until mid-morning.'

'Mother will insist on it not being talked about.'

'I'll do what I can.'

She walked him to the door while a little girl clung to her skirt.

'We're going out soon, darling. Go and ask Nana to dress you.'

Torrence was pacing the pavement outside the house. The little black police car cut a sad figure amid the long, glossy luxury cars.

'Quai des Orfèvres?'

'No, Ile Saint-Louis. Quai d'Orléans.'

The building was an old one, with a huge carriage entrance, but it was maintained like a valuable piece of furniture. The brasses, the banisters, the stairs, the walls were sparkling clean, without a speck of dust; even the concierge wore a black dress and a white apron, like a maid in an upper-class household.

'Do you have an appointment?'

'No. Madame Keller is expecting me.'

'One moment, please.'

The lodge was a little drawing room that smelled more of wax polish than of cooking. The concierge picked up the telephone.

'What's your name?'

'Detective Chief Inspector Maigret.'

'Hello, Berthe? Can you tell madame that a Detective Chief Inspector Maigret is asking to see her? . . . Yes, he's here. Can he come up? . . . Thanks . . . You may go up. Second floor, on the right.'

As he climbed the stairs, Maigret wondered if the Flemish barge was still moored at Quai des Célestins or if the statement had been signed and they were already travelling downstream towards Rouen. The door opened without his needing to ring. The maid, who was young and pretty, looked Maigret up and down as if this was the first time in her life that she had seen a police officer in the flesh.

'This way. Let me take your hat.'

The apartment, which had very high ceilings, was decorated in baroque style, with lots of gilt and extravagantly carved furniture. Even from the hall, a chatter of budgerigars could be heard, and as the door to the drawing room was open, a huge cage was visible, containing about ten couples.

He waited some ten minutes, ending up lighting his pipe as a protest. True, he took it out of his mouth as soon as Madame Keller made her entrance. It was a shock to him to find her so slight, so frail and yet so young. She seemed barely ten years older than her daughter. She was dressed in black and white and had a fair complexion and eyes the colour of forget-me-nots.

'Jacqueline phoned me,' she said immediately, motioning Maigret to an armchair with a tall straight back, which was as uncomfortable as could be.

She herself sat down on a stool upholstered in old tapestry, holding herself erect, as she must have been taught at convent school.

'So you've found my husband.'

'We weren't looking for him,' he replied.

'I assume not. I can't see why you would have been looking for him. Every person is free to live his own life. Is it true that his life is in no danger, or did you just say that to my daughter to spare her?'

'Professor Magnin gives him an eighty per cent chance of recovery.'

'Magnin? I know him well. He's been here several times.'

'Did you know your husband was in Paris?'

'I knew it and didn't know it. Since he left for Gabon about twenty years ago, all I've ever had from him was two postcards. And that was right at the beginning of his time in Africa.'

She was making no pretence at being upset, looking him full in the face like a woman who is accustomed to all kinds of situations.

'Are you at least sure it's him?'

'Your daughter recognized him.'

He held out the identity card with the photograph. She went to fetch her glasses from a chest of drawers and looked closely at the photograph without any emotion being visible on her face.

'Jacqueline's right. Obviously, he's changed, but I, too, would swear it was François.' She looked up. 'Is it true he was living very near here?'

'Under Pont Marie.'

'And to think I cross that bridge several times a week! I have a friend who lives just on the other side of the Seine. Madame Lambois. You probably know the name. Her husband—'

Maigret didn't wait to find out what important position Madame Lambois' husband occupied.

'Have you seen your husband since he left Mulhouse?'

'No, never.'

'Has he ever written or telephoned?'

'Apart from those two postcards, I've never had any news of him. Not directly, anyway.'

'What about indirectly?'

'Occasionally at the houses of friends I've met a former governor of Gabon, Pérignon, who once asked me if I was related to a doctor named Keller.'

'What did you reply?'

'I told him the truth . . . He seemed embarrassed . . . I had to pry information out of him. Then he admitted to me that François hadn't found what he was looking for over there.'

'What was he looking for?'

'He was an idealist, if you know what I mean. He wasn't cut out for modern life. After his disappointment in Mulhouse . . .'

Maigret expressed surprise.

'Didn't my daughter tell you? True, she was very young and saw so little of her father! Instead of building up the kind of practice he deserved . . . Will you have a cup of tea? No? Excuse me for having mine in front of you, but it's my teatime.'

She rang.

'My tea, Berthe.'

'For one?'

'Yes . . . What can I offer you, inspector? A glass of whisky? . . . Nothing? As you wish . . . Where was I? Oh yes. Didn't someone once write a novel called *The Doctor of the Poor*? Or was it *The Country Doctor*? Well, my husband was a kind of doctor of the poor, and, if I hadn't had that inheritance from my aunt, we would have ended up as poor as them. Not that I resent him for it. It was just the way he was. His father . . . Well, never mind about that. Every family has its problems.'

The telephone rang.

'Will you excuse me? . . . Hello? . . . Yes, speaking . . . Alice? . . . Yes, my dear . . . I may be a little late . . . No, on the contrary, I'm fine. Have you seen Laure? . . . Will she be there? . . . I can't say any more, I have a visitor . . . I'll tell you all about it, yes . . . See you later.'

She came back to her place, smiling.

'That was the wife of the minister of the interior. Do you know her?'

Maigret merely shook his head and instinctively put his pipe back in his pocket. The budgerigars were getting on his nerves, and so were the interruptions. Now, it was the turn of the maid, who came in to serve the tea.

'He got it into his head to become a hospital doctor, and for two years he studied hard for the exams . . . If you know Mulhouse, they'll tell you it was a flagrant injustice. François was definitely the best, the cleverest. And I think he would have felt at home there . . . As always, it was the protégé of a bigwig who was appointed . . . Not that that was any reason to give it all up.'

'So it was because of that disappointment . . .'

'I assume so. I saw so little of him! When he was at home, he would shut himself in his surgery. He'd always been a bit eccentric, but from then on it was as if he'd gone a bit crazy . . . I don't want to speak ill of him. It didn't even occur to me to get a divorce, even though he suggested it in his letter.'

'Did he drink?'

'Did my daughter tell you that?'

'No.'

'He started drinking, yes. Mind you, I never saw him drunk. But he always had a bottle in his surgery and he was quite often seen coming out of the kind of little bistros that a man in his position doesn't usually frequent.'

'You started telling me about Gabon.'

'I think he wanted to be a kind of Dr Schweitzer, if you know what I mean. Going off to the bush to treat Negroes, building a hospital there, seeing as little as possible of white people, people of his class.'

'And he was disappointed?'

'From what the governor told me reluctantly, he managed to antagonize the colonial administration, and the big companies, too. Perhaps because of the climate, he drank more and more . . . Don't think I'm telling you this because I'm jealous. I've never been jealous . . . He lived in a native hut, with a black woman, and apparently had children with her.'

Maigret was looking at the budgerigars in the cage, through which a sunbeam passed.

'He was given to understand that he wasn't wanted there.'

'You mean he was expelled from Gabon?'

'More or less. I don't know exactly how these things work, and the governor was quite vague about it all. But anyway, he left.'

'How long ago was it that a friend of yours met him on Boulevard Saint-Michel?'

'My daughter told you that, too, did she? Mind you, I can't be certain. The man was wearing a sandwich board advertising a local restaurant. He looked like François and apparently jumped when my friend called him by his name.'

'Did he speak to him?'

'François looked at him as if he'd never seen him before. That's all I know.'

'As I told your daughter earlier, I can't ask you to come and identify him right now, because his face is covered in bandages. But as soon as there's any improvement . . .'

'Don't you think it'll be painful?'

'For whom?'

'I'm thinking of him.'

'We have to be sure of his identity.'

'I'm pretty much certain, if only because of the scar. It was a Sunday in August . . .'

'I know.'

'In that case, I don't see what else I could possibly tell you.'

He stood up, anxious to be outside and no longer have to hear the chatter of the budgerigars.

'I suppose the newspapers—'

'The newspapers will say as little about it as possible, I promise.'

'It's not so much for me as for my son-in-law. In business, it's always unpleasant to . . . Mind you, he knows all about it and has been very understanding . . . Are you sure you won't have a drink?'

'Thank you, no.'

Once out in the street, he said to Torrence:

'Where can we find a nice quiet bistro? I'm incredibly thirsty!'

A glass of cold beer, with lots of foam.

They found the bistro, which was as quiet and shaded as they could have wished for, but unfortunately the beer was warm and flat.

4.

'The list is on your desk,' said Lucas, who had done a meticulous job, as usual.

There were even several lists, all typewritten. The first was of the miscellaneous objects found under Pont Marie – the specialist from Criminal Records had classified them under the heading *Sundry Remains* – which constituted Doc's assets. All of it – the old crates, the pram, the blankets with holes in them, the newspapers, the frying pan, the mess tin, Bossuet's *Oraisons funèbres*, and so on – was now upstairs, in a corner of the lab.

The second list was of the clothes that Lucas had brought back from the Hôtel-Dieu. The third, and last, itemized the contents of the pockets.

Maigret preferred not to read it. It must have been a curious sight, watching him sit there in the light of the setting sun and open the brown paper bag the sergeant had used for these small objects. Didn't he look a little like a child opening a party bag expecting to find some treasure or other?

The first thing he took out and placed on his blotting pad was a battered stethoscope.

'It was in the right-hand pocket of the jacket,' Lucas commented. 'I checked at the hospital. It doesn't work any more.'

If that was so, why did François Keller have it on him? Was he hoping to repair it? Or was it just a last remaining symbol of his profession?

Next came a pocket knife that had three blades and a corkscrew with a cracked horn handle. Like the rest, it had probably come from some dustbin or other.

A briar pipe, its stem held together with wire.

'Left-hand pocket,' Lucas recited. 'It's still damp.'

Maigret sniffed it mechanically.

'No tobacco?' he asked.

'There are a few cigarette ends at the bottom of the bag. They were so soaked they're only mush.'

It was easy to imagine the man stopping on the pavement, bending down to pick up a cigarette end, removing the paper and stuffing the tobacco in his pipe. Maigret didn't show it, but deep down he was pleased that Doc was a pipe smoker. Neither his daughter nor his wife had mentioned that.

Nails and screws. To do what? The tramp must have picked them up on his rounds and stuffed them in his pocket without thinking what he would use them for, probably seeing them as good luck charms.

The proof of that was that there were three more objects that would have been even less useful to someone who sleeps on the riverbank and wraps his chest in newspaper to protect himself from the cold: three marbles, the kind of glass marbles with yellow, red, blue and green filaments in them that you exchange as a child for five or six ordinary marbles and like to see glimmering in the sun.

That was almost everything, apart from a few coins

and a leather pouch containing two fifty-franc notes that the water of the Seine had stuck together.

Maigret kept one of the marbles in his hand, rolling it between his fingers during the rest of the conversation.

'Did you take his prints?'

'The other patients really took an interest when I did that. I've been upstairs and tried to find a match.'

'Anything?'

'No. Keller has never had any dealings with the law.'

'Has he regained consciousness?'

'No. When I was there, his eyes were half open, but he didn't seem to see anything. He wheezes a bit when he breathes. Occasionally, he moans.'

Before going home, Maigret signed the mail. In spite of his anxious air, there was nevertheless a carefree quality in his mood to match the Paris sky that day. Was it inadvertently that he slipped one of the marbles in his pocket as he left his office?

It was Tuesday, which was the day for macaroni cheese. Apart from the beef stew on Thursdays, the menu of the other days varied from week to week, but for years now, for no particular reason, Tuesday dinner had been given over to macaroni cheese with finely chopped ham and, occasionally, an even more finely cut truffle.

Madame Maigret was also in a cheerful mood, and from the gleam in her eyes he knew that she had something to tell him. He didn't immediately let her know that he had seen Jacqueline Rousselet and Madame Keller.

'I'm hungry!'

She was waiting for his questions. He refrained from

asking them until they were both sitting at the table by the open window. The air was bluish, with still a few red streaks low in the sky.

'Did your sister call you back?'

'I think she did quite well. She must have spent the afternoon phoning round all her friends.'

She had a small sheet of paper with notes beside her place setting.

'Shall I tell you what she told me?'

The noises of the city formed a background to their conversation, and the beginning of the television news could be heard from their neighbours' apartment.

'Don't you want to catch the news?'

'I'd rather listen to you.'

Two or three times, as she spoke, he put his hand in his pocket and played with the marble.

'Why are you smiling?'

'No reason. I'm listening.'

'First of all, I know where the fortune Madame Keller's aunt left her comes from. It's quite a long story. Do you want me to tell you the whole thing?'

He nodded as he ate the crunchy macaroni.

'She was a nurse, still unmarried at the age of forty.'

'Did she live in Mulhouse?'

'No, Strasbourg. She was Madame Keller's mother's sister. Are you following this?'

'Yes.'

'She worked in a hospital where each of the consultants had a few rooms for his private patients. One day, just before the war, she had to take care of a man who later

66

became quite notorious in Alsace, a man named Lemke. He was a scrap-metal merchant and he was already rich, with quite a bad reputation. It was said that he was a money-lender on the side.'

'Did he marry her?'

'How did you know?'

He regretted spoiling her story.

'I can tell it from your face.'

'He married her, yes. Wait for the rest. During the war, he continued as a scrap-metal merchant. Inevitably, he worked with the Germans and amassed quite a fortune . . . Am I going on too long? Am I boring you?'

'On the contrary. What happened at the Liberation?'

'The Resistance went after Lemke. They wanted to force him to pay back his ill-gotten gains, then shoot him, but they couldn't find him. Nobody knows where he and his wife were hiding. Somehow they managed to get to Spain, and from there they were able to set sail for Argentina. A mill owner from Mulhouse met Lemke over there in the street . . . A little more macaroni?'

'Gladly. With some crust.'

'I don't know if he was still working, or if both of them were travelling for pleasure. One day, they took a plane for Brazil, and the plane crashed in the mountains. The crew and all the passengers died. And it's precisely because Lemke and his wife died in a crash that the inheritance went to Madame Keller, who wasn't expecting it. Normally, the money should have gone to the husband's family. Do you know why the Lemkes got nothing and the wife's niece got everything?'

Cheating, he shook his head. Actually, he did know why.

'Apparently, when a man and his wife are victims of the same accident and it's not possible to establish which of the two died first, the law assumes that the wife survived, even if only for a few moments. Doctors say that women are tougher and take longer to die! So the aunt inherited first, and then the fortune went to her niece . . . Phew!'

She was pleased with herself, quite proud in fact.

'When it comes down to it, it's partly because a nurse met a scrap-metal merchant in a hospital in Strasbourg and a plane crashed in the mountains in South America that Dr Keller became a tramp. If his wife hadn't become rich overnight, if they'd continued to live in Rue du Sauvage, and if . . . You see what I mean? Don't you think he would have stayed in Mulhouse?'

'It's possible.'

'I also have information about her, but I warn you it's just gossip and my sister can't vouch for any of it.'

'Tell me anyway.'

'She's an active little woman, always on the move, who loves social events and is constantly seeking out important people. With her husband gone, she had a field day, organizing dinner parties several times a week. That's how she caught the eye of Prefect Badet, who had a disabled wife who's since died. According to the gossips, she was his mistress, and she's had other lovers, too, including a general whose name I've forgotten.'

'I've met her.'

Was Madame Maigret disappointed? If she was, she didn't let it show.

'What's she like?'

'Just as you've described her. A bright, energetic little woman, very well groomed, who doesn't look her age and loves budgerigars.'

'What have budgerigars got to do with it?'

'Her apartment is full of them.'

'And she lives in Paris?'

'On Ile Saint-Louis, three hundred metres from Pont Marie, where her husband slept. By the way, he smoked a pipe.'

Between the macaroni and the salad, he had taken the marble from his pocket and let it roll across the tablecloth.

'What's that?'

'A marble. Doc had three of them.'

She was looking closely at her husband.

'You like him, don't you?'

'I think I'm beginning to understand him.'

'You understand how a man like him can become a tramp?'

'Perhaps. He lived in Africa, the only white man in a place a long way from any city or main road. There, too, he was disappointed.'

'Why?'

How easy would it have been to explain this to Madame Maigret, who had spent her life surrounded by order and cleanliness?

'What I'm trying to figure out,' he continued in a light tone, 'is what he could have been guilty of.'

She frowned.

'What do you mean? He's the one who was attacked and thrown in the Seine, isn't he?'

'He's the victim, that's true.'

'So why do you say—?'

'Criminologists, especially American criminologists, have a theory about it, one that's not as far-fetched as it seems.'

'What theory?'

'That, out of every ten crimes, there are at least eight where the victim shares a good deal of responsibility with the perpetrator.'

'I don't understand.'

He was looking at the marble as if spellbound.

'Let's take a woman and a jealous man having an argument. The man reprimands the woman, and she responds by taunting him.'

'I suppose it happens.'

'Let's suppose he's holding a knife, and he says to her, "Watch out. Next time, I'll kill you."'

'I suppose that happens, too.'

Not in her world!

'Suppose, now, that she replies, "You wouldn't dare. You're not capable of something like that."'

'I get the idea.'

'Well, in a lot of crimes of passion, there's something of that. You were just talking about Lemke, who made his fortune, half by money-lending, putting the screws on his customers, half by wheeling and dealing with the Germans. Would you have been surprised to learn he'd been murdered?'

'But this doctor—'

'Didn't seem to be hurting anyone. He lived under the bridges, drank red wine from the bottle and walked the streets with a sandwich board.'

'You see!'

'And yet someone walked down on to the riverbank during the night and, taking advantage of the fact that he was asleep, struck him a blow on the head that could have been fatal, after which he dragged him to the Seine, from where he was only fished out by a miracle. That someone had a motive. In other words, consciously or not, Doc had given him a motive to get rid of him.'

'Is he still in a coma?'

'Yes.'

'Are you hoping to get something out of him when he's able to talk?'

He shrugged and started filling his pipe. Soon afterwards, they switched off the light and sat there by the still open window.

It was a calm, pleasant evening, and despite long silences between them, they felt very close to one another.

When Maigret got to his office the following morning, the weather was as radiant as the day before. On the trees, the little green shoots had already given way to real leaves, still thin and tender.

Maigret had only just sat down at his desk when Lapointe came in. He was in a jovial mood.

'I have two customers for you, chief.'

He was as proud and impatient as Madame Maigret had been the previous evening.

'Where are they?'

'In the waiting room.'

'Who are they?'

'The owner of the red Peugeot and the friend who was with him on Monday night. Not that I can take credit for it. Contrary to what you might think, there aren't many red 403s in Paris, and only three with number plates that have two nines in them. One of them has been out of action for a week, being repaired, and the second one is in Cannes right now with its owner.'

'Have you questioned these men?'

'I only asked them two or three questions. I thought it best you see them yourself. Shall I bring them in?'

There was something mysterious in Lapointe's demeanour, as if he had another surprise for Maigret up his sleeve.

'Go ahead.'

He waited, sitting at his desk. He still had a multicoloured marble in his pocket, like a good luck charm.

'Monsieur Jean Guillot,' Lapointe announced, admitting the first of the two men.

He was a man in his forties, of medium height, dressed with a certain care.

'Monsieur Lucien Hardoin, industrial draughtsman.'

He was taller, thinner and a few years younger and, as Maigret was soon to discover, he stammered.

'Sit down, gentlemen. From what I gather, one of you owns a red Peugeot.'

It was Jean Guillot who raised his hand, not without a certain pride.

'That's my car,' he said. 'I bought it at the beginning of winter.'

'Where do you live, Monsieur Guillot?'

'Rue de Turenne, not far from Boulevard du Temple.'

'What's your profession?'

'Insurance agent.'

He was clearly a little overawed to be in an office of the Police Judiciaire and to be questioned by a detective chief inspector, but he didn't seem scared. He even looked around curiously, as if hoping to give his friends a detailed account later.

'And you, Monsieur Hardoin?'

'I l-l-live in the s-s-same b-b-building.'

'The floor above us,' Guillot helped him.

'Are you married?'

'B-b-bachelor.'

'I'm married with two children, a boy and a girl,' Guillot said, not waiting to be asked.

Lapointe, standing by the door, smiled vaguely. The two men, each on a chair with his hat in his lap, were like a double act.

'Are you friends?'

They replied as unanimously as Hardoin's stammer allowed:

'Very good friends.'

'Did you know François Keller?'

They looked at each other in surprise, as if hearing this name for the first time. It was Hardoin who asked:

'Wh-wh-who's that?'

'He used to be a doctor, in Mulhouse.'

'I've never set foot in Mulhouse,' Guillot said. 'Does he claim he knows me?'

'What were you doing on Monday night?'

'As I told your inspector, I had no idea it was forbidden to—'

'Just tell me exactly what you were doing.'

'When I got back from my rounds, about eight o'clock – I do the western suburbs – my wife took me aside so that the children shouldn't hear and told me that Nestor—'

'Who's Nestor?'

'Our dog. A Great Dane. He was twelve years old and very gentle with the children. He'd been with them since they were born, more or less. When they were babies, he would lie at the foot of the cradle, and I hardly dared approach.'

'So, your wife told you—'

He continued, imperturbably:

'I don't know if you've ever had a Great Dane. In general, they don't live as long as other dogs, I'm not sure why. And in later life, they have almost all the same ailments as humans. For some weeks, he'd been almost paralysed, and I'd suggested taking him to a vet and having him put down, but my wife didn't want to. When I got back on Monday, he was dying, and, because my wife didn't want the children to see, she'd been to fetch our friend Lucien, who helped her take him to his apartment.'

Maigret looked at Lapointe, who winked at him.

'I immediately went upstairs to Lucien's to see how the animal was. Poor Nestor was on his last legs. I phoned the vet's and was told he was at the theatre and wouldn't be back until midnight. We spent more than two hours watching the dog die. I sat down on the floor and he put his head in my lap. He kept getting these terrible convulsions.'

Hardoin nodded and tried to intervene.

'He . . . he . . .'

'He died at ten thirty,' Guillot cut in. 'I went downstairs to tell my wife. I stayed in the apartment, where the children were asleep, while she went up to see Nestor one last time. I had a bite to eat, because I hadn't had dinner. I confess that after that I drank two glasses of cognac to buck me up, and when my wife came back down, I took the bottle upstairs and offered some to Lucien, who was as upset as I was.'

A little tragedy, in other words, on the fringes of another tragedy.

'That was when we asked ourselves what we were going to do with the body. I've heard there's such a thing as a dogs' cemetery, but I suppose it must be expensive, and apart from that, I can't afford to lose a day's work to sort it all out. And my wife doesn't have time.'

'Anyway,' Maigret said.

'Anyway . . .'

The word hung there, Guillot having lost the thread of his thoughts.

'We . . . we . . . we . . .'

'We didn't want to dump him on a piece of waste ground either. Have you any idea how big a Great Dane is? Lying there in Lucien's dining room, he looked even bigger and more impressive. Anyway . . .'

He was pleased to get back to that point.

'Anyway, we decided to throw him in the Seine. I went back to our apartment to look for a potato sack. It wasn't big enough, and the paws stuck out. It wasn't easy taking him downstairs and putting him in the boot of the car.'

'What time was this?'

'Ten past eleven.'

'How do you know it was ten past eleven?'

'Because the concierge wasn't in bed yet. She saw us go by and asked us what had happened. I told her. The door to the lodge was open, and I automatically looked at the clock. It said ten past eleven.'

'You told her you were going to throw the dog in the Seine? Did you go straight to Quai des Célestins?'

'It was the nearest place.'

'It couldn't have taken you more than a few minutes to get there. I don't suppose you stopped on the way?'

'Not on the way there. We took the shortest route. It only took five minutes. I wasn't sure about driving the car down the ramp, but as nobody was about, I took the risk.'

'So it wasn't yet eleven thirty.'

'Definitely not . . . You'll see . . . We both took hold of the sack and tipped it over into the river.'

'Still without seeing anyone?'

'Yes.'

'Was there a barge nearby?'

'Yes, there was. We even saw a light on inside.'

'But you didn't see the bargee?'

'No.'

'You didn't go as far as Pont Marie?'

'We had no reason to go any further. We threw Nestor into the river as close to the car as possible.'

Hardoin was still nodding, occasionally opening his mouth to get a word in, then closing it again, discouraged.

'What happened next?'

'We left. Once we were back up—'

'You mean on Quai des Célestins?'

'Yes. I didn't feel terribly well and I remembered there wasn't any more cognac left in the bottle. It had been a trying evening. Nestor was almost part of the family. When we got to Rue de Turenne, I suggested to Lucien that we have a drink, and we stopped outside a bar on the corner of Rue des Francs-Bourgeois, right next to Place des Vosges.'

'You had more cognac?'

'Yes. There was a clock there, too, and I looked at it. The owner told me it was five minutes fast. It was eleven forty.'

He repeated, apologetically:

'I swear to you I didn't know it's forbidden. Put yourself in my shoes. Especially with the children. I wanted to spare them. They still don't know the dog is dead. We've told them he's run away but we may still find him.'

Without realizing it, Maigret had taken the marble out of his pocket and was fingering it.

'I assume you've told me the truth?'

'Why would I lie? If there's a fine to be paid, I'm ready to—'

'What time did you get home?'

The two men looked at each other with a touch of

embarrassment. Hardoin opened his mouth once again, but once again it was Guillot who replied.

'Late. About one in the morning.'

'The bar in Rue de Turenne stayed open until one in the morning?'

It was a neighbourhood that Maigret knew well, where everything closes at midnight, or even well before midnight.

'No. We went for a final drink on Place de la République.'

'Were you drunk?'

'You know how it is. You drink when you're in an emotional state. One drink leads to another . . .'

'You didn't go back to the river?'

Guillot assumed a surprised air and looked at his friend as if asking him to add his testimony.

'No! What for?'

Maigret turned to Lapointe.

'Take them next door and get down their statements . . . I'm grateful to you, gentlemen. Needless to say, everything you've told me will be checked.'

'I swear I told the truth.'

'M-m-me, too.'

It was like a farce. Maigret remained alone in his office, standing by the open window, the glass marble in his hand. He looked pensively at the Seine flowing beyond the trees, the boats passing, the bright splotches of the women's dresses on Pont Saint-Michel.

He finally sat down again and asked for the Hôtel-Dieu.

'Put me through to the head nurse of the surgery unit.'

Now that she had seen him with the big boss and had received instructions, she was all sweetness and light.

'I was just about to phone you, inspector. Professor Magnin has just examined the patient. He says he's much better than last night and he hopes that complications can be avoided. It's almost a miracle.'

'Has he regained consciousness?'

'Not completely, but he's starting to take an interest in what's around him. It's hard to know if he's aware of the state he's in or where he is.'

'Does he still have his bandages?'

'Not on the face.'

'Do you think he'll regain consciousness today?'

'It may happen at any moment. Do you want me to let you know as soon as he speaks?'

'No. I'm on my way.'

'Now?'

Now, yes. He was anxious to make the acquaintance of the man whom he had previously only seen with his head bandaged. He passed through the inspectors' office, where Lapointe was typing up the statements of the insurance man and his friend with the stammer.

'I'm going to the Hôtel-Dieu. I don't know when I'll be back.'

It wasn't far. He went there as if paying a neighbourly visit, unhurriedly, his pipe between his teeth, his hands behind his back, all kinds of undefined thoughts going round and round in his head.

He got to the Hôtel-Dieu just as Fat Léa, still in her pink

blouse, was moving away from the counter with a disappointed look on her face. She rushed over to him.

'You know, inspector, not only are they stopping me from seeing him, but they're refusing to tell me how he is. They almost called a policeman to have me thrown out. Have you heard anything?'

'I've just been told he's much better.'

'Do they think he'll pull through?'

'It seems likely.'

'Is he in a lot of pain?'

'I don't think he's aware of it. I assume they've given him injections.'

'Yesterday, some plain-clothes men came looking for his things. Were they your people?'

He replied in the affirmative, adding with a smile:

'Don't worry. He'll get it all back.'

'Do you have any idea yet who might have done it?'

'Do you?'

'I've been living by the river for fifteen years, and this is the first time I've known anyone to attack a tramp. I mean, we're perfectly harmless, you must know that as well as anyone.'

She liked the word so much that she repeated it:

'Harmless. There are never even any fights. We respect each other's freedom. If we didn't respect other people's freedom, why would we be sleeping under the bridges?'

He looked at her more closely now and noticed that her eyes were a little red, her complexion brighter than the day before.

'Have you been drinking?'

'Just enough to pick me up.'

'What do your friends say?'

'They don't say anything. When you've seen it all, there's no enjoyment in gossip.'

As Maigret was about to walk through the front door, she asked him:

'Can I wait for you to come out? I'd like to know how he is.'

'I may be a long time.'

'It doesn't matter. I might as well be here as anywhere else.'

She had regained her good humour and childlike smile.

'I don't suppose you have a cigarette?'

He showed her his pipe.

'A pinch of tobacco, then. If I can't smoke, I can chew . . .'

He took the lift at the same time as a patient lying on a stretcher and two nurses. On the third floor, he ran into the head nurse just as she was coming out of one of the wards.

'You know where it is. I'll be with you in a moment. I'm wanted in emergency.'

The patients in their beds turned to look at him, as they had the previous day. They seemed to recognize him already. He headed for Dr Keller's bed, his hat in his hand, and at last discovered a face with only a few plasters left on it.

The man had been shaved the day before and looked almost nothing like his photograph. His features were hollow, his complexion lacklustre, his lips thin and pale. What struck Maigret most was being suddenly confronted with his gaze.

Because there was no doubt about it: Doc was looking at him, and it wasn't the look of a man who is unaware of things.

It embarrassed him to remain silent. But on the other hand, he didn't know what to say. There was a chair beside the bed, and he sat down on it and asked awkwardly:

'Are you feeling better?'

He was sure that the words were not going to be lost in the fog, that they were registered and understood. But the eyes, still fixed on him, did not move and expressed nothing but complete indifference.

'Can you hear me, Dr Keller?'

It was the beginning of a long and dispiriting battle.

5.

Maigret rarely talked to his wife about a case while it was in progress. In fact, most of the time he didn't even discuss it with his closest colleagues, content merely to give his instructions. It was all part of the way he worked, trying to understand, to gradually immerse himself in the lives of people he hadn't known the day before.

'What do you think, Maigret?' he had often been asked by an examining magistrate when the prosecutor's office visited a crime scene or staged a reconstruction.

His invariable reply was well known at the Palais de Justice:

'I never think.'

And someone had retorted one day:

'He soaks it all in.'

It was true in a way. Words were too precise for him, which was why he preferred to keep quiet.

It was different this time, at least where Madame Maigret was concerned, perhaps because she had given him a hand, thanks to her sister who lived in Mulhouse. Sitting down at the table for lunch, he announced:

'I made Keller's acquaintance this morning.'

She was quite surprised. Not only because he was the first to speak of it, but because of his cheerful tone. 'Cheerful' wasn't quite the right word. Nor was 'jolly'. All the same, there was a touch of lightness, a kind of good humour in his voice and his eyes.

For once, the newspapers weren't harassing him, and the deputy prosecutor and the examining magistrate were leaving him in peace. A tramp had been assaulted under Pont Marie and thrown into the rising Seine, but he had miraculously survived, and Professor Magnin couldn't get over his powers of recovery.

In short, it was a crime without a victim, almost without a perpetrator, and nobody really cared about Doc, apart from Fat Léa and, perhaps, two or three other tramps.

Yet Maigret was devoting as much of his time to this case as he would to a drama keeping the whole of France agog. He seemed to be making it a personal matter, and from the way he had just announced his encounter with Keller, it was almost as if he was talking about someone he and his wife had been anxious to meet for a long time.

'Has he regained consciousness?' Madame Maigret asked, taking care not to show too much interest.

'Yes and no. He didn't say a word. He just looked at me, but I'm convinced he understood everything I said to him. The head nurse doesn't agree. She says he's still dazed by the drugs he's been given and that he's in the same state as a boxer getting up after a knockout.'

As he ate, he looked through the window and listened to the birds.

'Do you get the feeling he knows the person who attacked him?'

Maigret sighed and finally gave a slight smile that was

unlike him, a mocking smile whose mockery was aimed at himself.

'I have no idea. I'd find it hard to explain the feeling I got.'

He had seldom been as disorientated in his life as he had been that morning, at the Hôtel-Dieu, or quite as fascinated by a problem.

The conditions of the interview were already quite unfavourable. It had taken place in a ward with a dozen patients lying in their beds and three or four seated or standing by the window. Some were in pain, in a serious condition, bells rang constantly, and a nurse came and went, bending over this bed or that.

With a greater or lesser degree of insistence, everyone was watching Maigret sitting beside Keller, and they were all ears.

Last but not least, the head nurse would appear at the door from time to time and watch them with an uneasy, discontented air.

'You mustn't stay too long,' she had advised him. 'Avoid tiring him.'

Bent over the tramp, Maigret spoke in a low, gentle voice, in a kind of murmur.

'Can you hear me, Monsieur Keller? Do you remember what happened to you on Monday night, when you were lying under Pont Marie?'

Not a feature on the wounded man's face moved, but Maigret was only interested in his eyes, which expressed neither fear nor anxiety. They were faded grey eyes, eyes that had seen a lot and appeared worn out.

'Were you asleep when you were assaulted?'

Doc made no attempt to take his eyes off him, and a curious thing was happening: it wasn't Maigret who seemed to be studying Keller, but Keller who was studying Maigret.

This impression was so disturbing that Maigret felt the need to introduce himself.

'My name is Maigret. I'm in charge of the Crime Squad at the Police Judiciaire. I'm trying to understand what happened to you. I've seen your wife, your daughter, the bargees who took you out of the Seine . . .'

Doc hadn't reacted at the mention of his wife and daughter, but Maigret would have sworn there had been a gleam of irony in his eyes.

'Are you unable to speak?'

He didn't try to respond with a movement of the head, however slight, or a flicker of the eyelids.

'Are you aware that you're being spoken to?'

Oh, yes! Maigret was sure he wasn't mistaken. Not only was Keller aware of it, but he wasn't losing any nuance of the words uttered.

'Does it bother you that I'm questioning you in this ward where other patients can hear us?'

Then, as if to win the tramp over, he took the trouble to explain:

'I'd have liked you to have a private room. Unfortunately, that involves complicated administrative matters. We can't pay for a room like that on our budget.'

Paradoxically, things would have been easier if, instead of being the victim, the doctor had been the assailant, or simply a suspect. When it came to the victim, there was no provision.

'I'm going to be obliged to bring your wife here, because she needs to formally identify you. Would it upset you to see her again?'

Keller's lips moved a little but emitted no sound, and there was neither a grimace nor a smile.

'Do you feel well enough for me to ask her to come by this morning?'

The man made no objection, and Maigret took the opportunity to pause. He felt hot. It was stifling in this ward, with its smell of illness and medications.

'Can I make a phone call?' he went and asked the head nurse.

'Are you going to keep tormenting him?'

'His wife has to identify him. It'll only take a few minutes.'

All this he recounted as best he could to Madame Maigret, as they had lunch by the window.

'She was at home,' he went on. 'She promised to come immediately. I gave instructions downstairs for her to be admitted. Then I went for a walk in the corridor, and after a while Professor Magnin joined me.'

The two men had talked, standing by a window that looked out on the courtyard.

'Do you also think his mind has cleared?' Maigret had asked.

'It's possible. When I examined him earlier, I had the impression he knew what was going on around him. But medically, I can't yet give you a categorical answer. People imagine we're infallible and can answer every question. But most of the time we're just feeling our way. I've asked a neurologist to see him this afternoon.'

'I suppose it's difficult to put him in a private room?'

'It's not only difficult, it's impossible. Everything's full. In some departments, we've been forced to set up beds in the corridors . . . Or else we'd have to transfer him to a private clinic.'

'What if his wife suggested that?'

'Do you think he'd like it?'

It was highly unlikely. Keller hadn't chosen to leave home and live rough in order to again be dependent on his wife, all because of an assault.

Madame Keller emerged from the lift and looked around her, disorientated. Maigret went over to greet her.

'How is he?'

She wasn't too anxious or upset. The most obvious impression was that she felt out of place and was in a hurry to get back to her apartment on Ile Saint-Louis and her budgerigars.

'He's calm.'

'Has he regained consciousness?'

'I think so, but I can't prove it.'

'Should I talk to him?'

He let her walk ahead of him, and all the patients watched her as she advanced across the polished wooden floor of the ward. For her part, she was searching for her husband, and of her own accord she headed for the fifth bed, then stopped two or three metres from it, as if she didn't know what attitude to adopt.

Keller had seen her and was looking at her, still indifferent.

She was very well dressed in a beige shantung tailored suit, with a matching hat, and her perfume mingled with the smells of the ward.

'Do you recognize him?'

'It's him, yes. He's changed, but it's him.'

There was another silence, which was painful for all of them. She finally summoned up her courage and went closer. Nervously fingering the clasp of her handbag with her gloved hands, she said:

'It's me, François. I always thought I'd find you in such an unfortunate condition one of these days. Apparently, you're going to make a speedy recovery. I'd like to help you.'

What was he thinking, looking at her like that? For seventeen or eighteen years, he had been living in another world. It was rather as if he had resurfaced only to find himself face to face with a past he had fled.

There was no bitterness visible on his face. He merely looked at the woman who for a long time had been his wife, then turned his head slightly to make sure that Maigret was still there.

As Maigret put it now to his wife:

'I'd swear he was asking me to put an end to this confrontation.'

'You talk about him as if you've known him for a long time.'

Wasn't that true in a way? Maigret had never met Keller before, but hadn't he, in the course of his career, had the opportunity to hear the confessions of many men like him in the privacy of his office? Perhaps not such extreme cases. But the human problem was the same.

'She didn't insist on staying,' he recounted. 'Before leaving him, she almost opened her bag to take out some money. Fortunately, she didn't. In the corridor, she asked me, "Do you think he needs anything?" And, when I said no, she insisted, "Perhaps I could give the hospital director some money to help him out? He'd be better off in a private room." "There isn't one free," I told her. She accepted that. "What should I do?" "Nothing for the moment. I'll send an inspector to your apartment who'll get you to sign a paper acknowledging that you've identified this man as your husband." "What's the point, since it's him?" She finally left . . .'

They had finished eating and now sat with their coffees. Maigret had lit his pipe.

'Did you go back to the ward?'

'Yes. In spite of the reproachful looks I got from the head nurse.'

She had become a kind of personal enemy.

'Did he talk at all this time?'

'No. I was the only one talking, in a low voice, with an intern treating the patient in the next bed.'

'What did you say to him?'

For Madame Maigret, this conversation over coffee was almost miraculous. Usually, she barely knew what case her husband was dealing with. He would phone her to tell her he wouldn't be back for lunch or dinner, sometimes that he would be spending part of the night in his office or somewhere else, and mostly it was through the newspapers that she learned more.

'I can't remember what I said to him,' he replied, his face clouding over slightly. 'I was trying to gain his trust. I told him that Léa was waiting for me outside, I told him we'd put his things in a safe place and that he'd get them back when he left hospital. That seemed to please him. I also told him that he wouldn't have to see his wife again if he didn't want to, that she'd offered to pay for a private room for him, but there were none available. From a distance I must have looked as if I was saying the rosary. I said, "I suppose you'd rather stay here than go to a clinic?"'

'And he still didn't reply?'

Maigret was embarrassed.

'I know it's stupid, but I'm sure he agreed with me, that we understood each other. I tried to get back to the night of the assault. I asked him, "Were you asleep?" It was a bit like a cat and mouse game. I'm convinced he's decided once and for all not to say anything. And a man who was capable of living rough for so long is quite capable of keeping quiet.'

'Why would he keep quiet?'

'I have no idea.'

'To avoid accusing someone?'

'Perhaps.'

'Who?'

Shrugging his broad shoulders, Maigret stood up.

'If I knew that, I'd be God the Father. I feel like answering you the way Professor Magnin answered me: I can't perform miracles either.'

'So in the end, you didn't learn anything new?'
'No.'
That wasn't quite accurate. He was convinced that he had learned a lot about Doc. Although he hadn't yet started to really know him, there had nevertheless been some fleeting and somewhat mysterious contacts between them.

'There was one moment . . .'

He hesitated, as if afraid of being accused of childishness. Too bad! He needed to speak.

'There was one moment when I took the marble from my pocket. To tell the truth, I didn't do it consciously. I felt it in my hand, and it occurred to me to slip it into his. I probably looked a bit ridiculous. But in fact, he didn't need to look at it. He recognized it from the touch. Whatever the nurse says, I'm sure his face lit up, and there was a wicked, happy gleam in his eyes.'

'But he still didn't say anything?'

'That's another matter. He's not going to help me . . . He's made up his mind not to help me, not to say anything, and I'll have to discover the truth for myself.'

Was it the challenge that excited him? His wife had seldom seen him so lively, so fascinated by a case.

'Downstairs, I ran into Léa again. She was waiting for me outside, chewing my tobacco. I gave her the contents of my pouch.'

'You don't think she knows anything?'

'If she did, she'd tell me. There's more solidarity among these people than there is among normal people who live in houses. I'm sure they're questioning each other right now, conducting their little investigation on the fringes of mine . . . She did tell me one thing that might be interesting: that Keller hasn't always slept under Pont Marie and has only been a local, if I can put it that way, for the past two years.'

'Where did he live before?'

'Still on the banks of the Seine, but further upstream, on Quai de la Rapée, under Pont de Bercy.'

'Do they often change location like that?'

'No. It's as big a thing for them as moving house is for us. They each have their own corner and get quite attached to it.'

In the end, as if by way of reward, or to keep up his good mood, he poured himself a little glass of sloe gin. After which, he took his hat and kissed Madame Maigret.

'See you this evening.'

'Do you think you'll be back for dinner?'

He had no idea, any more than she did. To be honest, he hadn't the slightest idea what he was going to do.

Since morning, Torrence had been checking the statement of the insurance agent and his friend with the stammer. He had probably already questioned Madame Goulet, the concierge in Rue de Turenne, and the bistro owner on the corner of Rue des Francs-Bourgeois.

They would know soon enough if the story about the dog Nestor was true or completely made up. Even if it was true, it still wouldn't prove that the two men hadn't assaulted Doc.

For what reason, though? At this stage, Maigret couldn't see any.

But what reason would Madame Keller, for example, have had to have her husband thrown in the Seine? And by whom?

One day, when an unremarkable, penniless man had been murdered in similarly mysterious circumstances, he had said to the examining magistrate:

'Losers don't get killed.'

Nor do tramps. And yet someone had definitely tried to get rid of François Keller.

Maigret was on the platform of the bus, listening distractedly to the phrases whispered by a pair of lovers standing next to him, when a hypothesis occurred to him. It was the expression 'loser' that had made him think of it.

No sooner was he in his office than he asked to be put through to Madame Keller. She wasn't at home. The maid informed him that she was having lunch in town with a friend, but had no idea in which restaurant.

He next called Jacqueline Rousselet.

'I gather you've seen Mother. She phoned me last night, after your visit. She just called me again, less than an hour ago. So it really is my father.'

'There seems to be no doubt about his identity.'

'Do you still have no idea why he was assaulted? Are you sure it wasn't a fight?'

'Did your father get into fights?'

'He was the gentlest man in the world, at least in the days when I lived with him, and I think he would have let himself be beaten without retaliating.'

'Are you familiar with your mother's business affairs?'

'What business affairs?'

'When she married, she wasn't rich and had no idea she would be rich one day, and neither did your father. Given that, I wonder if they had the idea of drawing up a convention of separate assets. If they didn't, they would have married according to the convention of common assets, which means that your father could well lay claim to half of her fortune.'

'That's not the case,' she replied without hesitation.

'Are you sure?'

'Mother can confirm it. When I married my husband, we discussed it with the notary. My mother and father married under the convention of separate assets.'

'Might I ask the name of your notary?'

'Maître Prijean, in Rue de Bassano.'

'Many thanks.'

'Don't you want me to go to the hospital?'

'Would you like to?'

'I'm not sure he'd be pleased to see me. He didn't say anything to my mother. Apparently, he pretended not to recognize her.'

'It might be better to avoid it for the moment.'

Needing to give himself the illusion that he was doing something, he immediately asked to have Maître Prijean on the telephone. He had to argue for quite a long time and even threaten an order signed by the examining magistrate, since the notary claimed professional confidentiality.

'I'm only asking you to tell me if Monsieur and Madame Keller, from Mulhouse, were married under the convention of separate assets and if you've seen the papers.'

It ended with a fairly curt 'yes' before the call was cut short.

In other words, François Keller was indeed a loser who had no right to the fortune amassed by the scrap-metal merchant that had ended up in his wife's hands.

The switchboard operator was quite surprised when Maigret asked:

'Get me the lock at Suresnes.'

'The lock?'

'The lock, yes. Lock-keepers have telephones, don't they?'

'Very well, chief.'

He was eventually put through to the chief lock-keeper and introduced himself.

'I assume you keep a note of the boats that pass from one reach to another? . . . I'd like to locate a motor barge which must have passed through your lock late yesterday afternoon. It has a Flemish name. *De Zwarte Zwaan*.'

'I know it, yes. Two brothers, a little blonde woman and a baby. They passed the last sluice and spent the night below the gates.'

'Do you have any idea where they are right now?'

'Wait. They have a good diesel engine and they're taking advantage of the fact that the current is still quite strong.'

He could be heard making calculations, muttering to himself the names of towns and villages.

'Unless I'm very much mistaken, they must be a hundred kilometres further on by now, which would put them near Juziers. Anyway, there's a good chance they've passed Poissy. That depends on how long they had to wait at the Bougival lock and then at Carrière.'

A few moments later, Maigret was in the inspectors' office.

'Does anyone here know the Seine really well?'

A voice asked:

'Upstream or downstream?'

'Downstream. Near Poissy, probably even further.'

'I do! I have a little boat and I go all the way to Le Havre every year during the holidays. I'm particularly familiar with the Poissy area because that's where I keep the boat.'

It was Neveu who had spoken, a nondescript, conventional-looking inspector: Maigret had no idea he was such an outdoor person.

'Get a car from the courtyard. You can drive me there.'

Maigret had to keep him waiting, because just then Torrence returned and communicated the result of his inquiries.

'The dog did die on Monday night,' he confirmed. 'Madame Guillot still cries when she talks about it. The two men put the body in the boot of the car and went to throw it in the Seine. The owner of the bar in Rue de Turenne remembers them. They arrived just before closing time.'

'What time was that?'

'Just after eleven thirty. Some customers playing belote were just finishing their game, and the owner was waiting to lower the shutters. Madame Guillot also confirmed that her husband got back late, she doesn't know exactly when, because she'd fallen asleep, and that he was half drunk. She was quite embarrassed and felt she had to swear to me that he wasn't in the habit, that you had to put it down to the emotion.'

Maigret finally got in the car next to Neveu, and they set off in the direction of Porte d'Asnières.

'We can't follow the Seine all the way,' Neveu said. 'Are you sure the barge has passed Poissy?'

'According to the chief lock-keeper.'

On the road, they started seeing cars with their tops down, and some drivers had their companions' arms around their waists. People were planting flowers in their gardens. At one point, a woman in a light-blue dress was feeding her hens.

Eyes half closed, Maigret dozed, apparently indifferent to the landscape. Each time they caught a glimpse of the Seine, Neveu would say the name of the place where they were.

They passed several boats peacefully going up and down the river. Here, a woman was washing her linen on deck; there, another was holding the helm, a child of three or four sitting at her feet.

The car stopped at Meulan, where several barges were moored.

'What name did you say, chief?'

'*De Zwarte Zwaan*. It means Black Swan.'

Neveu got out of the car, crossed the quayside and started up a conversation with some bargees. From a distance, Maigret saw them gesticulating.

'They passed half an hour ago,' Neveu announced as he got back in behind the wheel. 'As they're doing a good ten kilometres an hour or even more, they should be in the Juziers area by now.'

It was soon after Juziers, opposite the island of Montalet, that they spotted the Belgian barge travelling downstream.

They drove another two or three hundred metres and stopped, and Maigret went and took up position on the riverbank. There, unafraid of looking ridiculous, he started waving his arms.

It was Hubert, the younger of the two brothers, who was at the wheel, a cigarette in his mouth. Recognizing Maigret, he went and leaned over the hatch and slowed the engine. A moment later, the long, thin figure of Jef Van Houtte appeared on deck, first his head, then his chest, finally the whole of his tall, lanky body.

'I have to talk to you,' Maigret shouted to them, his hands cupped round his mouth.

Jef signalled that he couldn't hear anything, because of the engine, and Maigret tried to explain that he had to stop.

They were in open country. About a kilometre away, they could see red and grey roofs, white walls, a petrol pump, a golden inn sign.

Hubert Van Houtte put the engine into reverse. The young woman now also put her head out through the hatch. It wasn't hard to guess that she was asking her husband what was going on.

The manoeuvre was quite muddled. From a distance, it looked as if the two men were at odds. Jef, the older, was pointing to the village, as if ordering his brother to go in that direction, while Hubert, at the helm, was already approaching the bank.

Unable to do otherwise, Jef finally threw a rope, which

Inspector Neveu caught, proud to show off his expertise as a sailor. There were mooring posts on the bank, and a few minutes later the barge came to a standstill.

'What is it you want now?' Jef called out, apparently in a temper.

There was a gap of several metres between the bank and the barge, and he made no move to lay down the gangplank.

'Do you think it's right to stop a boat, just like that? It's a good way to have an accident, let me tell you.'

'I need to talk to you,' Maigret replied.

'You talked to me as much as you wanted in Paris. I don't have anything else to tell you.'

'In that case, I'm obliged to summon you to my office.'

'What is this? You want me to go back to Paris without unloading my slates?'

Hubert, who was more accommodating, gestured to his brother to calm down. It was he who finally threw the gangplank towards the bank, walked across it like an acrobat and secured it.

'Don't take any notice of him, monsieur. It's true, what he says. You can't stop just anywhere.'

Maigret climbed on board. Deep down, he felt quite embarrassed, not knowing exactly what questions he was going to ask. Moreover, he was now in Seine-et-Oise, and according to regulations it was up to the Versailles police to question the Van Houttes, and then only if they had a judge's order.

'Are you going to keep us here long?'

'I don't know.'

'Because we're not going to spend the night here, you know. We still have time to get to Mantes before the sun goes down.'

'In that case, keep going.'

'You mean you want to come with us?'

'Why not?'

'Now I've seen everything!'

'Did you hear, Neveu? Continue in the car as far as Mantes.'

'What do you say to that, Hubert?'

'There's nothing we can do about it, Jef. When the police are involved, there's no point getting angry.'

They could still see the blonde head of the young woman at the level of the deck and hear a child's babble from below. As had been the case the day before, pleasant cooking smells rose from the living quarters.

The gangplank was removed. Before getting back in the car, Neveu loosened the ropes, sending bright sprays of water flying up from the river.

'Since you still have questions, go ahead.'

They heard again the panting of the engine and the noise of the water sliding against the hull.

Standing in the stern of the barge, Maigret slowly filled his pipe, still wondering what he was going to say.

6.

'You did tell me yesterday that the car was red, didn't you?'

'Yes, monsieur. As red as the red on that flag.'

He pointed to the black, yellow and red Belgian flag fluttering in the stern.

Hubert was at the helm, and the young blonde woman had joined the child inside. As for Jef, his face betrayed two contradictory feelings between which he seemed torn. On the one hand, Flemish hospitality dictated that he should welcome Maigret in the manner appropriate to anyone you received in your home, and even offer him a little glass of genever; on the other hand, he was still angry at being stopped in open country and he considered this new interrogation an affront to his dignity.

He kept his sly eyes fixed on the intruder, whose city suit and black hat stood out like a sore thumb on board the barge.

As for Maigret, he wasn't particularly at his ease and was still wondering how to tackle his difficult interlocutor. He had had a great deal of experience of these simple, not very intelligent men, who think you are taking advantage of their naivety and who, because they don't trust you, either become aggressive or withdraw into a stubborn silence.

It wasn't the first time that Maigret had conducted an

investigation on board a barge, although it hadn't happened for a long time. He particularly remembered what used to be called a stable boat, towed along the canals by a horse that spent the night on board with its carter.

Those boats were of wood and smelled good because of the resin with which they were periodically coated. The interior was neat and tidy, not unlike that of a suburban house.

Here, through the open door, the decor looked more bourgeois: solid oak furniture, rugs, vases on embroidered doilies, a multitude of shiny brasses.

'Where were you when you heard noises on the quayside? You were busy working on the engine, I think?'

Jef's light-coloured eyes were fixed on him. He looked as if he was still hesitating as to what attitude to adopt and fighting against his own anger.

'Listen, monsieur. Yesterday morning, you were there when the judge asked me all those questions. You asked me some yourself. And the little man who was with the judge wrote everything down. In the afternoon, he came back and made me sign a statement. Is that correct?'

'That's correct.'

'And now you come here and ask me the same thing. I don't think it's fair. Because if I make a mistake, you'll think I lied to you. I'm no intellectual, monsieur. I never had much schooling. Nor did Hubert. But we're both hard workers, and Anneke is also a working woman.'

'I'm only trying to check—'

'There's nothing to check. I was minding my own business on my boat, like you were in your house. A man was thrown in the water, and I jumped into the lifeboat to fish him out. I'm not asking for a reward, or congratulations. But that's no reason for you to come and pester me with questions. That's what I think, monsieur.'

'We tracked down the two men in the red car.'

Did Jef's face really cloud over, or did it just seem that way to Maigret?

'Well, then, you only have to ask them.'

'They claim it wasn't midnight, but eleven thirty, when they got out of the car on the riverbank.'

'Maybe their watches were slow, right?'

'We've checked their testimony. They next went to a bar in Rue de Turenne. It was eleven forty when they got there.'

Jef looked at his brother, who had turned to him quite abruptly.

'Do you think we could go inside?'

The cabin was quite spacious and served as both kitchen and dining room. A stew was simmering on the white enamel stove. Madame Van Houtte, who was breastfeeding the baby, rushed into one of the bedrooms, where Maigret just had time to glimpse a bed covered with a counterpane.

'You can sit down, right?'

Still hesitant, as if reluctant, he took from the buffet with its stained-glass doors a brown stoneware pitcher of genever and two thick-bottomed glasses.

Through the square windows, the trees on the riverbank could be seen, and occasionally the red roof of a villa. There was a fairly long silence, during which Jef remained standing, his glass in his hand. He finally took a swig, keeping it in his mouth for a time before swallowing it.

'Is he dead?' he asked at last.

'No. He's regained consciousness.'

'What does he say?'

It was Maigret's turn not to reply. He was looking at the embroidered curtains at the windows, the house plants in their copper flowerpot holder, the photograph on the wall in a gilded frame, showing a large, middle-aged man in a thick sweater and a sailor's cap.

He was the kind of character you see often on boats, thickset, with huge shoulders and a walrus moustache.

'Is that your father?'

'No, monsieur. That's Anneke's father.'

'Was your father also a bargee?'

'My father, monsieur, was a docker in Antwerp. And that isn't a job for a respectable man, if you know what I mean.'

'Is that why you became a bargee?'

'I started working on the barges at the age of thirteen, and nobody has ever complained about me.'

'Last night—'

Maigret thought he had softened him up with his indirect questions, but the man shook his head.

'No, monsieur, I'm not playing that game. You just have to read the paper again.'

'And what if I find out that your statement isn't accurate?'

'Well, that's up to you.'

'You saw the two men from the car come back from under Pont Marie?'

'Read the statement.'

'They say they didn't go past your barge.'

'People can say what they like, right?'

'They also say they didn't see anybody on the bank, and that all they did was throw a dead dog in the river.'

'It's not my fault if they call it a dog.'

The young woman came back without the child, whom she must have put to bed. She said a few words in Flemish to her husband. He nodded, and she started straining the soup.

The barge was slowing down. Maigret wondered if they had already arrived, but through the window he soon saw a tugboat, followed by three barges, laboriously moving upstream. They passed under a bridge.

'Does this boat belong to you?'

'It's mine and Anneke's.'

'Isn't your brother a co-proprietor?'

'What does that mean?'

'Doesn't he own a share of it?'

'No, monsieur. The boat is mine and Anneke's.'

'In other words, your brother is your employee?'

'Yes, monsieur.'

Maigret was getting used to his accent, and to his endless repetition of 'monsieur' and 'right?' It was clear, from the way the young woman looked at them, that she only understood a few words of French and was wondering what on earth these two men were saying to each other.

'Since when?'

'About two years.'

'Did he work on another boat before that? In France?'

'Like us, he worked in Belgium and France. It depends on the cargo.'

'Why did you send for him?'

'Because I needed someone, right? It's a big boat, you know.'

'And before that?'

'Before what?'

'Before you sent for your brother?'

Maigret was advancing only little by little, looking for the most innocent questions in order to avoid his interlocutor taking offence again.

'I don't understand.'

'Was there someone else helping you?'

'Of course.'

Before answering, he had glanced at his wife, as if to make sure she hadn't understood.

'Who was he?'

Jef refilled the glasses, to give himself time to think.

'It was me,' he finally declared.

'You were the hand?'

'I was the mechanic.'

'Who was the skipper?'

'I wonder if you really have the right to ask me all these questions. A man's private life is his own business. And I'm Belgian, monsieur.'

The more heated he became, the stronger his accent.

'It's not what I call manners. All this is my business, and just because I'm Flemish doesn't mean you can play about with my things.'

It took Maigret a few moments to grasp the meaning of this expression, and he couldn't help smiling.

'I could come back with an interpreter and question your wife.'

'I won't allow Anneke to be bothered.'

'You'll have to if I bring an order from the judge. I'm wondering now if it would be simpler to take the two of you back to Paris.'

'And what would become of the boat? No, I'm sure you have no right to do that.'

'Why don't you just answer my questions?'

Van Houtte lowered his head a little and threw Maigret a sly look, like a schoolboy plotting a prank.

'Because it's none of your business.'

So far, he had been right. Maigret had no serious reason to harass him like this. He was following his intuition. Coming on board near Juziers, he had been struck by the bargee's attitude.

He wasn't exactly the same man he had been in Paris. Jef had been surprised to see Maigret on the riverbank and he had had a strong reaction. Since then, he had remained suspicious, withdrawn, without that gleam in his eye, that sense of humour he had demonstrated on Quai des Célestins.

'Do you want me to take you back?'

'You'd have to have a reason. There are laws.'

'The reason is that you're refusing to answer routine questions.'

They could still hear the gasping of the engine and glimpse Hubert's long legs standing by the helm.

'Because you're trying to confuse me.'

'I'm not trying to confuse you, only to establish the truth.'

'What truth?'

He kept advancing and retreating, one moment sure of his rights, the next visibly worried.

'When did you buy this barge?'

'I didn't buy it.'

'But it does belong to you?'

'Yes, monsieur, it belongs to me and it belongs to my wife.'

'In other words, it was by marrying her that you became the owner? The boat was hers?'

'Is that so remarkable? We were married legally, in front of the mayor and the priest.'

'Before that, her father was the skipper of the *Zwarte Zwaan*?'

'Yes, monsieur. Old Willems.'

'Didn't he have any other children?'

'No, monsieur.'

'What happened to his wife?'

'She'd been dead for a year.'

'Were you already on board?'

'Yes, monsieur.'

'For how long?'

'Willems hired me when his wife died. That was at Oudenaarde.'

'Were you working on another barge?'

'Yes, monsieur. The *Drie Gebrouders*.'

'Why did you change?'

'Because the *Drie Gebrouders* was an old barge that almost never came to France and mostly carried coal.'

'And you don't like carrying coal?'

'It's dirty.'

'So you've been on this boat for about three years. How old was Anneke at the time?'

Hearing her name, she looked at them curiously.

'Eighteen, right?'

'Her mother had just died.'

'Yes, monsieur. At Oudenaarde, I already told you.'

He listened to the noise of the engine, looked at the bank, then went and said a few words to his brother, who was slowing down to pass under a railway bridge.

Patiently, Maigret picked up the thread, tenuous as it was.

'Until then, the boat had been a family affair, but with the mother dead, they needed someone. Is that correct?'

'That's correct.'

'You were in charge of the engine.'

'The engine and all the rest. On a barge, you have to do everything.'

'Did you immediately fall in love with Anneke?'

'That's a personal question, right, monsieur? It's my business and it's her business.'

'When did you get married?'

'Next month will make two years.'

'When did Willems die? Is that his picture on the wall?'

'Yes, that's him.'

'When did he die?'

'Six weeks before the wedding.'

More and more, Maigret had the impression that he was advancing at a discouragingly slow pace, going round in ever smaller circles, and he needed to summon all his patience in order not to scare Van Houtte.

'Had the banns been published by the time Willems died?'

'Where we come from, the banns are published three weeks before the wedding. I don't know how it is in France.'

'But the wedding was already planned?'

'Presumably, since we got married.'

'Would you like to ask your wife that question?'

'Why would I ask her a question like that?'

'If you don't, I'll be obliged to ask the question myself through an interpreter.'

'Well, then . . .'

He was about to say: 'Do it!'

And Maigret would have been quite ill at ease. They were in Seine-et-Oise, where he had no right to conduct such an interrogation.

Luckily, Van Houtte thought better of it and spoke to his wife in their language. She blushed, surprised, looked at her husband, then at her guest, and said something which she accompanied with a slight smile.

'Do you mind translating?'

'What she's saying is that we'd been in love for a long time.'

'For nearly a year, by then?'

'Almost immediately.'

'In other words, it started as soon as you were living on board.'

III

'What's wrong with—'

'What I'm wondering is whether Willems knew about it,' Maigret cut in.

Jef didn't reply.

'I suppose that at first anyway, like most lovers, you hid it from him?'

Once again, Jef looked outside.

'We're nearly there. My brother needs me on deck.'

Maigret followed him up there, and indeed, they could see the quayside at Mantes-la-Jolie, the bridge, a dozen barges moored in the small harbour.

The engine turned in slow motion. When they put it in reverse, there were big bubbles around the tiller. People were looking at them from the other boats, and it was a boy of about twelve who caught the mooring rope.

It was obvious that the presence of Maigret, in his city suit, a hat with a brim on his head, excited curiosity.

From one of the barges, someone called to Jef in Flemish, and he replied in the same language, still concentrating on the manoeuvre.

On the quayside, next to the little black police car, and not far from a huge pile of bricks, Inspector Neveu was standing, smoking a cigarette.

'I hope you'll leave us in peace now? It's nearly time for supper. People like us get up at five in the morning.'

'You haven't answered my question.'

'What question?'

'You haven't told me if Willems knew about your relationship with his daughter.'

'Did I marry her or not?'

'You married her once he'd died.'

'Is it my fault he died?'

'Was he ill for a long time?'

They were again standing in the stern of the boat, and Hubert was listening to them with a frown on his face.

'He was never ill in his life, unless it's an illness to be drunk every night.'

Maigret might have been mistaken, but it seemed to him that Hubert was surprised by the turn their conversation had taken and was looking at his brother strangely.

'Did he die of delirium tremens?'

'What's that?'

'The way most drunks end up. They have an attack that—'

'He didn't have an attack. He was drunk and he fell.'

'In the water?'

Jef didn't seem to appreciate the presence of his brother, who was still listening to them.

'In the water, yes.'

'Did this happen in France?'

He nodded.

'In Paris?'

'That's where he drank the most.'

'Why?'

'Because he'd meet up with a woman, I don't know where, and they'd both spend part of the night getting drunk.'

'Do you know this woman?'

'I don't know her name.'

'Or where she lives?'
'No.'
'But you saw her with him?'
'I met them, and once I saw them go into a hotel. There's no point telling Anneke.'
'Doesn't she know how her father died?'
'She knows how he died, but she's never been told about the woman.'
'Would you recognize her?'
'I might. I'm not sure.'
'Was she with him when he had his accident?'
'I don't know.'
'How did it happen?'
'I can't tell you that, because I wasn't there.'
'Where were you?'
'In my bed.'
'And Anneke?'
'In her bed.'
'What time was it?'
He replied reluctantly, but he replied.
'Past two in the morning.'
'Did Willems often come back that late?'
'In Paris, yes, because of that woman.'
'What happened?'
'I told you. He fell.'
'Crossing the gangplank?'
'I suppose so.'
'Was it in summer?'
'No, in December.'
'Did you hear the noise when he fell?'

'I heard something hit the hull.'

'Any cries?'

'He didn't cry out.'

'Did you rush to help him?'

'Of course.'

'Without taking time to get dressed?'

'I put on a pair of trousers.'

'Did Anneke also hear?'

'Not immediately. She woke up when I went up on deck.'

'When you went up, or when you were already there?'

Jef's eyes filled with something close to hate.

'Ask her. How do you expect me to remember?'

'Did you see Willems in the water?'

'I didn't see anything at all. I could only hear movement.'

'Could he swim?'

'He knew how to swim. But I suppose that time he couldn't.'

'Did you get in the lifeboat, as you did on Monday night?'

'Yes, monsieur.'

'Did you manage to get him out of the water?'

'Not before at least ten minutes went by, because every time I tried to grab hold of him, he would go under.'

'Was Anneke on deck?'

'Yes, monsieur.'

'So by the time you fished him out, he was dead?'

'I didn't know yet that he was dead. What I know is that he was purple.'

'Did you call a doctor, the police?'

'Yes, monsieur. Do you have any more questions?'

'Where did it happen?'

'In Paris, I told you.'

'Where in Paris?'

'We'd loaded wine in Mâcon and we were unloading it on Quai de la Rapée.'

Maigret managed to show no surprise, no satisfaction. It was as if he suddenly became more affable, as if his nerves were no longer on edge.

'I think I've almost finished. Willems drowned one night on Quai de la Rapée, when you were sleeping on board and his daughter was also asleep. Is that it?'

Jef blinked.

'About a month later, you married Anneke.'

'It wouldn't have been decent to live together on board without getting married.'

'When did you send for your brother?'

'Immediately. Three or four days after . . .'

'After your wedding?'

'No. After the accident.'

Although the sun had disappeared behind the pink roofs, it was still light, with a slightly unreal, almost disturbing brightness.

Hubert was still standing motionless by the helm, seemingly lost in thought.

'I don't suppose you know anything?'

'About what?'

'About what happened on Monday evening?'

'I was busy dancing in Rue de Lappe.'

'What about the death of Willems?'

'I was in Belgium when I got the telegram.'

'Have we finished yet?' Jef Van Houtte asked impatiently. 'Can we go and have our supper?'

To which Maigret replied very calmly, in a detached tone:

'I'm afraid not.'

That caused a shock. Hubert quickly raised his head and looked, not at Maigret, but at his brother. As for Jef, he asked, more aggressively than ever:

'And do you mind telling me why I can't have my supper?'

'Because I'm planning to take you back to Paris.'

'You have no right to do that.'

'I could send for a summons. It'd be here in an hour, signed by the examining magistrate.'

'Why, may I ask?'

'So that we can continue this interrogation elsewhere.'

'I've said what I had to say.'

'And also so that I can bring you face to face with the tramp you pulled out of the Seine on Monday night.'

Jef turned to his brother as if appealing to him for help.

'Hubert, do you think the inspector has the right . . .'

But Hubert said nothing.

'Are you going to take me in your car?'

He had spotted it on the quayside, with Neveu next to it, and he pointed.

'And when will I be allowed to get back to my boat?'

'Maybe tomorrow.'

'And if not tomorrow?'

'In that case, there's a good chance you'll never come back.'

'What are you saying?'

He clenched his fists, and for a moment Maigret thought he was going to throw himself on him.

'What about my wife? And my child? What are all these stories you're making up? I'll inform my consul.'

'That's your privilege.'

'This is a joke, right?'

He still couldn't believe it.

'You can't just come to a man's boat and arrest him when he's done nothing.'

'I'm not arresting you.'

'What else do you call it?'

'I'm taking you to Paris to confront you with a witness who can't be moved.'

'I don't even know the man. I pulled him out of the water because he was calling for help. If I'd known . . .'

His wife appeared and asked him a question in Flemish. He replied volubly. She looked at the three men in turn, then spoke again. Maigret would have sworn that she was advising her husband to follow him.

'Where are you planning to let me sleep?'

'We'll give you a bed at Quai des Orfèvres.'

'In prison?'

'No. At the Police Judiciaire.'

'Can I at least change my clothes?'

Maigret let him do so, and he disappeared below deck with his wife. Left alone with Maigret, Hubert still said nothing, just looked vaguely at the passers-by and the cars on the riverbank. Maigret said nothing either. He felt exhausted after this meandering interrogation, during which, discouraged, he had constantly thought he would get nowhere.

It was Hubert who spoke first, in a conciliatory tone.

'Don't take any notice. He's a hothead, but he's not a bad man.'

'Did Willems know about his relationship with his daughter?'

'On board a boat, it isn't easy to hide.'

'Do you think he liked the idea of their getting married?'

'I wasn't there.'

'And do you think he fell in the water, crossing the gangplank one night when he was drunk?'

'It often happens, you know. A lot of bargees die that way.'

Below, there was an argument going on, Anneke's voice imploring while her husband's betrayed anger. Was he again threatening not to go with Maigret?

It was she who won, because Jef finally came back on deck, his hair neatly combed and still wet. He was wearing a white shirt that brought out the colour of his complexion, an almost new blue suit, a striped tie and black shoes, as if on his way to Sunday Mass.

He exchanged a few more words in his language with his brother, without looking at Maigret, then got off the barge and headed for the black car, beside which the inspector was waiting.

Maigret opened the door. Neveu watched both of them in surprise.

'Where to, chief?'

'Quai des Orfèvres.'

It was dark by the end of the ride. The headlights lit up now the trees, now the houses of a village, finally the grey streets of the outer suburbs.

Maigret smoked his pipe in a corner, not saying a word. Jef Van Houtte didn't open his mouth either. Impressed by this uncommon silence, Neveu wondered what could have happened.

He ventured to ask:

'Did you get what you wanted, chief?'

Receiving no answer, he now contented himself with driving the car.

It was eight in the evening by the time they entered the courtyard of the Police Judiciaire. Only a few windows were still lighted, but old Joseph was still at his post.

In the inspectors' office, there were only three or four men, including Lapointe, who was typing.

'Send for some sandwiches and beer.'

'For how many people?'

'Two. No, three, because I'm going to need you. Are you free?'

'Yes, chief.'

Standing there in the middle of Maigret's office, the bargee seemed taller and thinner, his features more defined.

'You can sit down, Monsieur Van Houtte.'

The 'monsieur' made Jef frown, as if he saw it as a threat.

'We'll bring you some sandwiches.'

'And when can I see the consul?'

'Tomorrow morning.'

Sitting at his desk, Maigret called his wife on the telephone.

'I won't be back for dinner . . . No . . . It's possible I'll be here part of the night.'

She must have wanted to ask him lots of questions, but knowing the interest her husband took in the tramp, she contented herself with just one.

'Is he dead?'

'No.'

She didn't ask him if he had arrested someone. Given that he was phoning from his office and foresaw staying there part of the night, it meant that an interrogation was under way or soon would be.

'Good night.'

He looked at Jef irritably.

'I asked you to sit down.'

It bothered him to see that big body motionless in the middle of the office.

'What if I don't want to sit down? I'm allowed to stand, right?'

Maigret merely sighed and waited patiently for the waiter from the Brasserie Dauphine to arrive with the beer and sandwiches.

7.

These nights, which eight times out of ten ended with confessions, had finished up acquiring their own rules, their own traditions even, like stage plays that are performed hundreds of times.

The inspectors on duty in the various departments had immediately grasped what was happening, as had the waiter from the Brasserie Dauphine who had brought up the sandwiches and beer.

Jef Van Houtte's bad mood, his more or less contained anger, hadn't stopped him from eating with gusto, or from drinking his first beer in one go, all the while watching Maigret out of the corner of his eye.

Whether out of defiance or protest, he deliberately ate messily, chewing loudly with his mouth open, spitting a little hard piece of ham on the floor, just as he would have spat it in the water.

Calm and benign in appearance, Maigret pretended not to notice these provocations and let him prowl around the office like a caged animal.

Had he done the right thing or not? The most difficult thing in an investigation is often to know when exactly to go for broke. Not that there are any hard and fast rules. It doesn't depend on this or that element. It's only a matter of intuition.

He had sometimes gone on the offensive without having any genuine clue and succeeded in a few hours. At other times, on the contrary, holding all the aces and with a dozen witnesses, it had taken the whole night.

It was important, too, to find the right tone, which was different with every suspect, and it was this tone he was looking for as he finished eating, observing the bargee.

'Would you like some more sandwiches?'

'What I'd like is to get back to my boat and my wife, that's what I'd like!'

He would eventually get tired of walking around in circles and sit down. He was the kind of a man there was no point in rushing, and the method to adopt with him was doubtless that of the 'singing session': start gently, without accusing him; let him get away with a first, unimportant contradiction, then another, some small mistake, and gradually entangle him until he was trapped.

The two men were alone, Maigret having entrusted Lapointe with an errand.

'Listen, Van Houtte—'

'I've been listening to you for hours, right?'

'The reason it's lasted so long may be because you're not being honest in your answers.'

'You're going to call me a liar, maybe?'

'I'm not accusing you of lying, just of not telling me everything.'

'What would you do if I started asking you questions about your wife and children?'

'You had a tough childhood. Did your mother care much about you?'

'So now it's my mother's turn? Let me tell you this. My mother died when I was only five years old. She was an honest woman, a saint, who if she's looking at me right now from up in Heaven . . .'

Maigret stopped himself from reacting and retained his grave expression.

'Did your father marry again?'

'My father was another story. He drank too much.'

'How old were you when you started earning your own living?'

'I started out at thirteen, I told you.'

'Do you have any other brothers apart from Hubert? What about sisters?'

'I have one sister. What of it?'

'Nothing. We're getting acquainted.'

'Well, if we're getting acquainted, I should ask you questions, too.'

'I don't see any harm in that.'

'You say that because you're in your office and you think you're all-powerful.'

Maigret had known from the start that this was going to be long and difficult, because Van Houtte was not an intelligent man. Invariably, it was the idiots they had most trouble with because they dug their heels in, refused to answer, unhesitatingly denied what they had stated an hour earlier and didn't get flustered when it was pointed out that they had contradicted themselves.

With an intelligent suspect, it was often enough to discover the flaw in his argument, his system, and everything quickly collapsed.

'I don't think I'm wrong in thinking that you're a hard worker.'

A sidelong glance, heavy with mistrust.

'Sure, I've always worked hard.'

'Some of your bosses must have taken advantage of your goodwill and your youth. Then one day, you met Louis Willems, who drank like your father . . .'

Motionless in the middle of the room, Jef was looking at him with the air of an animal sensing danger but not yet sure how it is going to be attacked.

'I'm convinced that if it hadn't been for Anneke, you wouldn't have stayed on board the *Zwarte Zwaan* and would have found another boat.'

'Madame Willems was a good woman, too.'

'And she wasn't proud and domineering like her husband.'

'Who told you he was proud?'

'Wasn't he?'

'He was the boss, the skipper, and he made sure everyone knew it.'

'I'd wager that Madame Willems, if she'd lived, wouldn't have objected to your marrying her daughter.'

He might have been an idiot, but he had the instincts of a wild animal, and this time Maigret had gone too fast.

'That's your story, is it? Well, I can also make up stories!'

'It's your story, as I imagine it, at the risk of getting it wrong.'

'And too bad for me if, because you're wrong, you throw me in prison.'

'Hear me out. You had a difficult childhood. When you were still young, you worked as hard as a grown man. Then you meet Anneke and she looks at you in a different way from how you've been looked at before. She considers you, not as someone who's on board to take care of all the chores and get yelled at, but as a human being. It's only natural you should fall in love with her. Her mother, if she'd lived, would probably have supported your relationship.'

At last! The man sat down, not yet on a chair, but on the arm of an armchair, which was already progress.

'What of it? It's a nice story, you know.'

'Unfortunately, Madame Willems had died. You were alone on board with her husband and Anneke, in contact with her all day long, and I'd swear that Willems kept his eye on you.'

'If you say so.'

'He was the owner of a fine boat, and he didn't want his daughter to marry a penniless young man. When he drank in the evening he turned unpleasant, violent.'

Maigret was regaining his caution and wouldn't take his eyes off Jef's.

'Do you think I'd let a man raise his hand to me?'

'I'm sure you wouldn't. Only, it wasn't you he raised his hand to. It was his daughter. I wonder if he didn't catch the two of you.'

It was better to let a few seconds go by. The silence weighed heavily, while Maigret's pipe smoked gently.

'You told me something interesting earlier. It was particularly in Paris that Willems went out in the evening, because he'd meet up with a lady friend and get drunk with her. In other places, he'd drink on board or in a tavern near where he was moored. Like all bargees who, as you told me, get up before dawn, he must have gone to bed early. In Paris, you had the opportunity to be alone, Anneke and you.'

There was the sound of footsteps and voices in the next office. Lapointe half opened the door.

'It's done, chief.'

'Later.'

And the 'singing session' continued, the office now full of smoke.

'It's possible that one night he came back earlier than usual and found you in each other's arms. If that's what happened, he definitely would have lost his temper. And his tempers must have been terrible. Maybe he threw you out and beat his daughter.'

'That's your story,' Jef repeated in an ironic tone.

'It's the story I'd choose if I were in your shoes. Because, in that case, Willems's death would be almost an accident.'

'It was an accident.'

'I said almost. I'm not even saying that you helped him to fall in the water. He was drunk. He was staggering. Was it raining that night?'

'Yes.'

'You see! So the gangplank was slippery. The only thing you did wrong was not to help him immediately. Unless it was more serious than that, and you pushed him. It all happened two years ago, and the police report refers to it as an accident, not a murder.'

'Then why are you so determined to pin it on me?'

'I'm only trying to explain. Suppose now that someone saw you push Willems in the water. Someone you didn't know was there, who was on the riverbank. He'd have been able to tell the police that you stayed on the deck of the barge for quite a long time before jumping into the lifeboat, in order to give your boss time to die.'

'And Anneke? Maybe she also saw it all and didn't say anything?'

'At two o'clock in the morning, it's quite likely she was asleep. In any case, the man who saw you, and who was living under Pont de Bercy at the time, didn't say anything to the police. Tramps don't much like getting involved in other people's business. They don't see the world like everyone else and they have their own idea of justice. You were able to marry Anneke and, as you needed someone with you to steer the boat, you got your brother to join you from Belgium. At last you were happy. You'd become the boss now, the skipper. Since then, you've been through Paris several times and I suspect you avoided mooring anywhere near Pont de Bercy.'

'No, monsieur! I've moored there at least three times.'

'Because the tramp wasn't there any more. Tramps also move house, and yours settled under Pont Marie. On Monday, he recognized the *Zwarte Zwaan*. He recognized you. What I wonder is . . .'

He pretended to be pursuing a new idea.

'What do you wonder?'

'I wonder if you noticed him on Quai de la Rapée when Willems was pulled out of the water. Yes, you would definitely have had to see him. He approached, but didn't say anything. On Monday, when he started prowling around your boat, you realized he might talk. It's not unlikely that he threatened to do so.'

Maigret didn't believe that. It wasn't Doc's style. For the moment, it was necessary for his story.

'You were afraid. It occurred to you that what had happened to Willems might well happen to someone else, almost in the same way.'

'And I threw him in the water, is that it?'

'Let's say you pushed him.'

Once again, Jef was standing, calmer than before, harder.

'No, monsieur! You'll never make me admit such a thing. It isn't the truth.'

'Well, if I got some of the details wrong, then tell me.'

'I've already said it.'

'What?'

'It was written down in black and white by the little man who was with the magistrate.'

'You stated that you heard a noise about midnight.'

'If I said it, it's true.'

'You also said that two men, one of them wearing a light-coloured raincoat, emerged from under Pont Marie at that moment and ran to a red car.'

'It *was* red.'

'So they walked past your barge.'

Van Houtte didn't react. Maigret went to the door and opened it.

'Come in, gentlemen.'

Lapointe had gone to fetch the insurance agent and his friend with the stammer from their homes. He had found them playing belote with Madame Guillot, and they had followed him without protest. Guillot was wearing the same yellowish raincoat as on Monday evening.

'Are these the two men who left in the red car?'

'It's not the same thing, seeing people at night on a badly lit riverbank and seeing them in an office.'

'They match the description you gave us.'

Jef shook his head, still refusing to express an opinion.

'They were definitely on Quai des Célestins that night. Can you tell us what you were doing there, Monsieur Guillot?'

'We drove the car down the ramp.'

'How far is this ramp from the bridge?'

'More than a hundred metres.'

'You stopped the car right at the foot of the ramp?'

'Yes.'

'And then?'

'We went to get the dog from the boot.'

'Was he heavy?'

'Nestor weighed more than I do. Seventy kilos two months ago, the last time we weighed him at the butcher's.'

'Was there a barge at the quayside?'

'Yes.'

'You both went with your load to Pont Marie?'

Hardoin opened his mouth to object, but luckily his friend intervened before him.

'Why should we have gone all the way to Pont Marie?'

'Because this gentleman here says you did.'

'He saw us go to Pont Marie?'

'Not exactly. He saw you come back from there.'

The two men looked at each other.

'He can't have seen us walking past his barge, because we threw the dog in the river behind the barge. I was even afraid the sack would get caught in the tiller. I waited for a moment to make sure the current would take it downstream.'

'Do you hear that, Jef?'

To which Jef replied, unfazed:

'That's his story, right? You told your story. And maybe there'll be other stories. It isn't my fault if—'

'What time was it, Monsieur Guillot?'

Unable to resign himself to a silent role, Hardoin blurted out:

'Elev-v-ven th-th—'

'Eleven thirty,' his friend cut in. 'The proof of that is that we were in the bar in Rue de Turenne by eleven forty.'

'Is your car red?'

'It's a red 403, yes.'

'With two nines in the licence number?'

'7949 LF 75. If you want to see the registration . . .'

'Would you like to go down to the courtyard and identify the car, Monsieur Van Houtte?'

'The only thing I'd like to do is go back to my wife.'

'How do you explain these contradictions?'

'It's up to you to explain them. It's not my job.'

'You know the mistake you made?'

'Yes. Pulling that man out of the water.'

'First, yes. But you didn't do that deliberately.'

'What do you mean, I didn't do it deliberately? Do you think I was sleepwalking when I untied the lifeboat, took the pole and tried to—'

'You're forgetting that someone else had heard the tramp yelling. Willems hadn't cried out, probably because he choked as soon as he hit the cold water. When it came to Doc, you took the precaution of knocking him out first. You assumed he was dead, or as good as, at any rate that he'd be unable to make it, given the strong current. You were unpleasantly surprised when you heard his cries for help. And you'd have let him yell as much as he liked if you hadn't heard another voice, the skipper of the *Poitou*. He saw you standing on the deck of your boat. So you thought it wise to play the rescuer.'

Jef merely shrugged.

'When I told you a moment ago that you made a mistake, that's not what I was referring to. I was thinking of your story. Because you saw fit to tell a story, in order to divert suspicion. It was a clever story you put together . . .'

The insurance agent and his friend looked in awe at Maigret and the bargee in turn, realizing at last that a man's head was at stake.

'At eleven thirty, you weren't busy working on your engine, as you claimed, you were in a place from which you could see the riverbank, either the cabin or somewhere on the deck of the boat. Otherwise, you wouldn't have seen the red car. You were watching when the dog was thrown in the river. You remembered it when the police asked you what had happened. You assumed the car wouldn't be traced, so you mentioned two men coming back from under Pont Marie.'

'I'm letting you talk, right? They can tell whatever story they like. You can tell whatever story *you* like.'

Maigret again walked over to the door.

'Come in, Monsieur Goulet.'

Once again, it was Lapointe who had gone to fetch the skipper of the *Poitou*, from which sand was still being unloaded on Quai des Célestins.

'What time was it when you heard cries coming from the Seine?'

'About midnight.'

'Can you be more precise than that?'

'No.'

'But it was later than eleven thirty?'

'Definitely. When it was all over, I mean by the time the body was hoisted on to the bank and the policeman arrived, it was twelve thirty. I think the policeman wrote the time down in his notebook. Well, it certainly hadn't been more than half an hour since—'

'What do you say to that, Van Houtte?'

'Me? Nothing at all, right? He has his story.'

'And the policeman?'

'The policeman has his story, too.'

By ten in the evening, the three witnesses had left, and another tray of sandwiches and beer had been brought up from the Brasserie Dauphine. Maigret went to the adjoining office and said to Lapointe:

'All yours.'

'What should I ask him?'

'Anything you like.'

It was routine. Sometimes three or four officers took turns during the night, asking more or less the same questions in a different way, gradually wearing down the suspect's resistance.

'Hello? Get my wife on the line, please.'

Madame Maigret wasn't yet in bed.

'I'd advise you not to wait up for me.'

'You sound tired. A tough one?'

She sensed the discouragement in his voice.

'He'll deny it to the end and won't give us anything to pin on him. He's the finest specimen of a stubborn idiot I've ever dealt with.'

'What about Doc?'

'I'm going to inquire after him now.'

His next call was indeed to the Hôtel-Dieu. He was put through to the night nurse from surgery.

'He's asleep. No, he's in no pain. The professor dropped by to see him after dinner and says he's out of danger.'

'Has he said anything?'

'Before going to sleep, he asked me for a drink.'

'Did he say anything else?'

'No. He took his sedative and closed his eyes.'

Maigret walked up and down the corridor for half an hour, letting Lapointe have a go. He could hear the murmur of the young inspector's voice from behind the door. Then he went back into his office and found Jef Van Houtte at last sitting on a chair, his big hands folded on his lap.

Lapointe's expression was clear evidence that he had got nowhere, while Jef's was one of mockery.

'How long is this going on for?' he asked, watching Maigret resume his seat. 'Don't forget you promised to get hold of the consul. I'll tell him everything you've done, and it'll be in the Belgian newspapers.'

'Listen to me, Van Houtte.'

'I've been listening to you for hours, but you keep repeating the same thing.' He pointed to Lapointe. 'And this one, too. Do you have others waiting behind the door to come in and ask me questions?'

'Maybe.'

'I'll give them the same answers.'

'You've contradicted yourself several times.'

'What if I have? Wouldn't you contradict yourself if you were in my shoes?'

'You heard the witnesses.'

'The witnesses say one thing, I say another. That doesn't mean I'm the one who's lying. I've worked all my life. Ask any of the bargees what they think of Jef Van Houtte. Not a single one will have anything bad to say about me.'

And Maigret started all over again, determined not to let go, recalling the case of a man as tough as Jef who had suddenly caved in at the sixteenth hour, just when he was about to give up.

Tonight was one of his most exhausting nights. Twice, he went into the next office, and Lapointe took his place. By the end, there were no more sandwiches, no more beer, and they had the impression there were only the three of them left, like ghosts, in the deserted premises of the Police Judiciaire, where the cleaning women were sweeping the corridors.

'It's impossible for you to have seen the two men walk past your barge.'

'The difference between us is that I was there and you weren't.'

'You heard them.'

'Everyone talks.'

'Not that I'm accusing you of premeditation.'

'What does that mean?'

'I'm not claiming you knew in advance that you were going to kill him.'

'Who? Willems or the fellow I pulled out of the water? Because now there are two of them, right? And tomorrow, maybe there'll be three, or four, or five. It's easy enough for you to add more.'

At three o'clock, an exhausted Maigret decided to give up. For once, it was he, and not the suspect, who was at the end of his tether.

'Let's call it a day,' he grunted, getting to his feet.

'So, can I go back to my wife?'

'Not yet.'

'Are you going to make me sleep in a cell?'

'You'll sleep here, on a camp bed in one of the offices.'

While Lapointe led him there, Maigret left headquarters and walked the deserted streets with his hands in his pockets. He didn't find a taxi until he got to Châtelet.

He crept into the bedroom. Madame Maigret shifted in bed and mumbled in a sleepy voice:

'Is that you?'

As if it might have been someone else!

'What time is it?'

'Four o'clock.'

'Has he confessed?'

'No.'

'Do you think it's him?'

'In all conscience, I'm sure it is.'

'But you've had to let him go?'

'Not yet.'

'Would you like me to make you something to eat?'

He wasn't hungry, but he poured himself a glass of brandy before going to bed, despite which it took him a good half-hour to get to sleep.

He wouldn't forget the Belgian bargee in a hurry!

8.

It was Torrence who went with them that morning, because Lapointe had spent the rest of the night at Quai des Orfèvres. Previously, Maigret had had quite a long telephone conversation with Professor Magnin.

'I'm certain he's been fully conscious since last night,' the professor declared. 'The only thing I ask is that you don't tire him. Don't forget he's had a serious shock and will take some weeks to recover completely.'

The three of them walked by the river in the sun, Van Houtte between Maigret and Torrence, and they might have been taken for friends out for a stroll and savouring a fine spring morning.

For want of a razor, Van Houtte hadn't shaved, and his face was covered in blond hairs that glistened in the sun.

Opposite the Palais de Justice, they had stopped in a bar for coffee and croissants. Jef had scoffed seven of these as calmly as could be.

He must have thought they were taking him to Pont Marie for some kind of reconstruction and was surprised to be led into the grey courtyard of the Hôtel-Dieu, then along the corridors of the hospital.

Although he frowned from time to time, he seemed unperturbed.

'Can we go in?' Maigret asked the head nurse, who

looked his companion up and down and eventually shrugged her shoulders. This was all too much for her, and she had given up trying to understand.

For Maigret, it was the last chance. He was the first to walk into the ward, where, as had happened the previous day, the patients watched him. He was followed by Jef, whom he was partly hiding, while Torrence brought up the rear.

Doc watched him coming without any evident curiosity. When he saw Jef, there was no change in his demeanour.

As for Jef, he was no more flustered than he had been during the night. He stood there, looking with indifference at the sight of a hospital ward, which must have been unusual to him.

The expected shock did not materialize.

'Come forwards, Jef.'

'What do you want me to do now?'

'Come here.'

'All right. And now?'

'Do you recognize him?'

'I suppose he's the one who was in the water, right? Only, that night, he had a beard.'

'But you recognize him anyway?'

'I think so.'

'What about you, Monsieur Keller?'

Maigret was almost holding his breath, his eyes fixed on the tramp, who was looking at him and only slowly made up his mind to turn to the bargee.

'Do you recognize him?'

Did Keller hesitate? Maigret would have sworn he did. There was a long moment of expectation, until the former doctor from Mulhouse again looked at Maigret without showing any emotion.

'Do you recognize him?'

He contained himself, almost furious suddenly with this man who, he knew now, had decided to say nothing.

The proof of this was that there was something like the shadow of a smile on the tramp's face, a wicked gleam in his eyes.

His lips half opened, and he muttered:

'No.'

'He's one of the two bargees who took you out of the Seine.'

'Thank you,' he uttered in a barely audible voice.

'I'm almost sure he was also the one who hit you on the head and threw you in the water.'

Silence. Doc remained motionless, life only in his eyes.

'Do you still not recognize him?'

It was all the more impressive in that this exchange was being conducted in low voices, with two rows of patients in their beds spying on them and pricking up their ears.

'You don't want to talk?'

Keller had still not moved.

'You know, though, why he attacked you.'

There was a touch more curiosity in the eyes now. The tramp seemed surprised that Maigret had learned as much as he had.

'It goes back to two years ago, when you were still sleeping under Pont de Bercy. One night . . . Can you hear me?'

He made a sign that he could hear.

'One night in December, you witnessed a scene in which this man was involved.'

Keller seemed to be wondering again what decision to take.

'Another man, the skipper of the barge near which you were lying, was pushed into the river. That one wasn't saved . . .'

Silence still, followed finally by complete indifference on the tramp's face.

'Is that true? Seeing you again on Monday on Quai des Célestins, the killer was afraid you would talk.'

The head moved slightly, with effort, just enough for Keller to be able to see Jef Van Houtte.

But there was still no hate, no resentment in his eyes. The only thing visible in them was a certain curiosity.

Maigret realized he wouldn't get anything else from the tramp, and when the head nurse came and announced that they had stayed long enough, he didn't insist.

In the corridor, the bargee raised his head high.

'That got you a long way, didn't it?'

He was right. He was the winner of this match.

'I can also make up stories,' he said triumphantly.

And Maigret couldn't help muttering under his breath: 'Shut up!'

While Jef waited with Torrence at Quai des Orfèvres, Maigret spent nearly two hours in Dantziger's office. The magistrate had phoned the deputy prosecutor and asked him to join them, and Maigret told both men the whole story, in detail.

Dantziger took notes in pencil, and when the account was over, he sighed:

'To sum up, we don't have a single shred of evidence against him.'

'No, we don't.'

'Apart from the matter of the times not matching. Any good lawyer would wipe the floor with that argument.'

'I know.'

'Do you still have any hope of getting a confession?'

'None at all,' Maigret admitted.

'The tramp will maintain his silence?'

'I'm convinced he will.'

'Why do you think he's chosen to react in this way?'

That was harder to explain, especially to people who had never known the small world of those who live under bridges.

'Yes, for what reason?' the deputy prosecutor cut in. 'I mean, he almost died. In my opinion, he ought to . . .'

In the opinion of a deputy prosecutor, who probably lived in an apartment in Passy with his wife and children, organized weekly bridge parties and was concerned about his own advancement and how much he earned compared with the others.

Not in the opinion of a tramp.

'After all, there is something called justice.'

Indeed there was. But those who are not afraid to sleep under bridges in the middle of winter, wrapped in old newspapers to keep warm, didn't bother with that kind of justice.

'Do you understand him?'

Maigret hesitated to answer yes, because they would probably have given him funny looks.

'Well, he doesn't believe that a court trial, speeches by the prosecution and the defence, a jury verdict and prison are such important things.'

What would the two men have said if he had told them how he had slipped a marble into the tramp's hand? Or if he had simply told them that the former Dr Keller, whose wife lived on Ile Saint-Louis and whose daughter had married a big manufacturer of pharmaceutical products, had glass marbles in his pockets like a ten-year-old boy?

'Is he still demanding to see his consul?'

They were talking about Jef again now.

After a glance at the deputy prosecutor, the magistrate said hesitantly:

'As the case currently stands, I don't think I can sign an arrest warrant against him. From what you tell me, it wouldn't be any use for me to question him myself.'

Indeed not. What Maigret had been unable to obtain, the magistrate certainly wouldn't.

'Well?'

Well, as Maigret had known when he arrived, the game was lost. All they could do was release Van Houtte, who might well demand an apology.

'I'm sorry, Maigret, but as things stand . . .'

'I know.'

It was always an unpleasant process. This wasn't the first time it had happened – and always with idiots!

'I apologize, gentlemen,' he said in a low voice as he left them.

A little later, back in his office, he repeated:

'I apologize, Monsieur Van Houtte. Or rather, I apologize as a matter of form. But I want you to know that my opinion hasn't changed. I'm convinced you killed your employer, Louis Willems, and that you did everything you could to get rid of the tramp, who was an inconvenient witness. That said, there's nothing to stop you from going back to your barge, your wife and your baby. Goodbye, Monsieur Van Houtte.'

What happened, though, was that the bargee did not object, merely looked at Maigret with a certain surprise and, once he was at the door, held out his hand at the end of his long arm and muttered:

'Anyone can make a mistake, right?'

Maigret ignored the hand. Within five minutes, he was gritting his teeth and throwing himself back into other cases in progress.

In the weeks that followed, they carried out painstaking searches, both in Bercy and around Pont Marie, questioned lots of people, and received reports from the Belgian police that were added, pointlessly, to other reports.

As for Maigret, for three months he was often seen on Quai des Célestins, his pipe between his teeth, his hands in his pockets, as if out for a stroll. Doc had finally left hospital and had gone back to his corner under the arch of the bridge. He had been given back his things.

Maigret sometimes stopped by him, as if by chance. Their conversations were brief.

'How are you?'

'Fine.'

'Does your wound still hurt?'

'I feel a little dizzy from time to time.'

Even though they avoided talking about the case, Keller knew perfectly well what Maigret had come for, and Maigret knew he knew. It had become a kind of game between them.

A little game that lasted until the height of summer, when, one morning, Maigret stopped in front of the tramp, who was eating a crust of bread and drinking red wine.

'How are you?'

'Fine!'

Did François Keller decide that Maigret had waited long enough? He was looking in the direction of a moored barge, a Belgian barge that wasn't the *Zwarte Zwaan*, but looked like it.

'Those people have a nice life,' he remarked.

And pointing at two fair-haired children playing on deck, he added:

'Especially them.'

Maigret looked him in the eyes, gravely, sensing that something was to follow.

'Life isn't easy for anybody,' the tramp went on.

'Nor is death.'

'What's impossible is to judge.'

They understood each other.

'Thank you,' Maigret murmured. At last he knew.

'Don't mention it. I haven't said anything . . .'

And Doc added, like Jef:

'Right?'

Indeed, he hadn't said anything. He refused to judge. He wouldn't testify.

All the same, Maigret was able to announce to his wife, casually, in the middle of lunch:

'You remember the barge and the tramp?'

'Yes. Are there any developments?'

'I wasn't wrong.'

'So you've arrested him?'

He shook his head.

'Oh, no! Unless he does something careless, which would surprise me, we'll never arrest him.'

'Did Doc talk to you?'

'In a way, yes.'

With his eyes much more than with words. They had understood one another, and Maigret smiled at the memory of the complicity that had been established between them for a moment, under Pont Marie.

INSPECTOR MAIGRET

OTHER TITLES IN THE SERIES

MAIGRET IN COURT
GEORGES SIMENON

'They suddenly found themselves in an impersonal world, where everyday words no longer seemed to mean anything, where the most mundane details were translated into unintelligible formulae. The judges' black gowns, the ermine, the prosecutor's red robe further added to the impression of a ceremony set in stone where the individual counted for nothing.'

When Maigret is called to testify in court and reveals his doubts about a picture-framer accused of double murder, his actions have tragic consequences that he could never have foreseen.

Translated by Ros Schwartz

www.penguin.com

Other Titles in the Series

MAIGRET AND THE OLD PEOPLE
GEORGES SIMENON

'He had seldom been so perplexed by human beings. Would a psychiatrist, a teacher or a novelist ... have been better placed to understand characters who had suddenly materialized from another century?'

The violent death of a distinguished former ambassador, the Count of Saint-Hilaire – an old man without political secrets or enemies – confounds Inspector Maigret, until a bundle of letters promises to uncover the tragic truth.

Translated by Shaun Whiteside

www.penguin.com

OTHER TITLES IN THE SERIES

MAIGRET AND THE LAZY BURGLAR
GEORGES SIMENON

'Sullenly, he got dressed. Why, whenever he was woken on a winter night like this, did the coffee have a particular taste? The smell of the apartment was different, too.'

When his superiors dismiss the death of a burglar as part of Paris's gang wars, Inspector Maigret defies their orders and tries to discover what really happened to the quiet, likeable crook he had known for years.

Translated by Howard Curtis

www.penguin.com

OTHER TITLES IN THE SERIES

MAIGRET AND THE GOOD PEOPLE OF MONTPARNASSE
GEORGES SIMENON

'Why all of a sudden did this shock him? He was annoyed with himself for being shocked. He felt as if he had been sucked into the bourgeois, almost edifying, atmosphere that surrounded those people, "good people" so everyone kept telling him.'

When a seemingly decent man is found shot dead in his family home, Maigret must look beyond the calm, well-to-do exterior of his exemplary life to find the truth.

Translated by Ros Schwartz

www.penguin.com

Other Titles in the Series

MAIGRET AND THE SATURDAY CALLER
GEORGES SIMENON

'I followed you. Last Saturday, I nearly came up to you in the street, then I thought that wasn't the right place. Not for the kind of conversation I wanted to have. Not in your office either. Perhaps you'll understand . . .'

When Maigret is followed home by a man who confesses he intends to commit a crime, he tries to dissuade this strange visitor, but a subsequent disappearance casts an ominous new light on events.

Translated by Sian Reynolds

www.penguin.com

INSPECTOR MAIGRET

Other Titles in the Series

Pietr the Latvian
The Late Monsieur Gallet
The Hanged Man of Saint-Pholien
The Carter of La Providence
The Yellow Dog
Night at the Crossroads
A Crime in Holland
The Grand Banks Café
A Man's Head
The Dancer at the Gai-Moulin
The Two-Penny Bar
The Shadow Puppet
The Saint-Fiacre Affair
Mr Hire's Engagement
The Flemish House
The Madman of Bergerac
The Misty Harbour
Liberty Bar
Lock No. 1
Maigret
Cécile is Dead
The Cellars of the Majestic
The Judge's House
Signed, Picpus
Inspector Cadaver
Félicie
Maigret Gets Angry
Maigret in New York
Maigret's Holiday
Maigret's Dead Man
Maigret's First Case

My Friend Maigret
Maigret at the Coroner's
Maigret and the Old Lady
Madame Maigret's Friend
Maigret's Memoirs
Maigret at Picratt's
Maigret Takes a Room
Maigret and the Tall Woman
Maigret, Lognon and the Gangsters
Maigret's Revolver
Maigret and the Man on the Bench
Maigret is Afraid
Maigret's Mistake
Maigret Goes to School
Maigret and the Dead Girl
Maigret and the Minister
Maigret and the Headless Corpse
Maigret Sets a Trap
Maigret's Failure
Maigret Enjoys Himself
Maigret Travels
Maigret's Doubts
Maigret and the Reluctant Witness
Maigret's Secret
Maigret in Court
Maigret and the Old People
Maigret and the Lazy Burglar
Maigret and the Good People of Montparnasse
Maigret and the Saturday Caller
Maigret and the Tramp

And more to follow

www.penguin.com